T0328743

THE DEMON IS STRONGER
THAN YOU THINK. . . .

"Who are you?" I ask.

"You know who I am."

I take a deep breath. I'm very frightened now. "I want you to tell me," I insist.

"You trust the Healer," the girl says. She sighs and shakes her head. "Can't you smell the Demon's stench on him?"

"What are you saying?"

"You'll find out soon enough. You have to."

Tears flow down my cheeks. "I don't understand."

"Time is short, Julia. Time is very, very short. The Demon is stronger than you think."

I shake my head. And in the flickering light of the fire, I can see something else now: an hourglass . . . an old hourglass filled with black sand. It's very tall— taller than a person. It's standing right beside the girl. It's almost empty. The last of the blackness tumbles swiftly through the narrow funnel. . . .

"Remember what you've seen," the girl says. "Time is running out."

About the Author

Daniel Parker is the author of over twenty books for children and young adults. He lives in New York City with his wife, a dog, and a psychotic cat named Bootsie. He is a Leo. When he isn't writing, he is tirelessly traveling the world on a doomed mission to achieve rock-and-roll stardom. As of this date, his musical credits include the composition of bluegrass sound-track numbers for the film *The Grave* (starring a bloated Anthony Michael Hall) and a brief stint performing live rap music to baffled Filipino audiences in Hong Kong. Mr. Parker once worked in a cheese shop. He was fired.

COUNT DOWN

by
Daniel Parker

Simon & Schuster
www.SimonSays.com/countdown/

If you purchased this book without a cover you should be aware that this book is stolen property. It was reported as "unsold and destroyed" to the publisher and neither the author nor the publisher has received any payment for this "stripped book."

First Aladdin Paperbacks edition June 1999

Copyright © 1999 by 17th Street Productions,
a division of Daniel Weiss Associates, Inc.
and Daniel Ehrenhaft
Cover art copyright © 1999 by 17th Street Productions,
a division of Daniel Weiss Associates, Inc.

 Produced by 17th Street Productions,
a division of Daniel Weiss Associates, Inc.
33 West 17th Street, New York, NY 10011

Cover design by Mike Rivilis

Aladdin Paperbacks
An imprint of Simon & Schuster
Children's Publishing Division
1230 Avenue of the Americas
New York, NY 10020

All rights reserved, including the right of
reproduction in whole or in part in any form.
The text of this book was set in 10.5 point Rotis Serif.
Printed and bound in the United States of America
10 9 8 7 6 5 4 3 2 1

Library of Congress Cataloging-in-Publication Data
Parker, Daniel, 1970-
July / by Daniel Parker. — 1st Aladdin Paperbacks ed.
p.   cm. — (Countdown) ; 7)
Summary: As the Demon Lilith continues to grow in strength,
some of the world's teenage survivors worry about finding a cure for the plague
that has killed all the adults, while others try to party themselves to death.
ISBN 978-1-4814-2592-6
[1. Supernatural—Fiction.] I. Title.
II. Series: Parker, Daniel, 1970-   Countdown ; 7.
PZ7.P2243Jn   1999
[Fic]—dc21

To The Noopies

JULY

The Ancient Scroll
of the Scribes:

In the seventh lunar cycle,
During the months of Tammuz
and Av in the year 5759,
The earth will again
be shielded from the sun,
And all but a few of the Seers will be blinded.
But those who do see the light of
truth will come to an understanding
That the Chosen One needs their help.
That the days of hope are numbered.
For at this time the traitor starts
to fall under the Demon's spell.
Confused, lost, and without hope,
The traitor brings woe to the Chosen One.
The False Prophet leaves his kingdom,
Led astray by servants of the Demon,
And begins a journey that will
unite the forces of darkness.

Truth never rests in honor,
now that man understands a sign
to be or to battle a poor coward.
Seven seventeen ninety-nine.

The countdown has started . . .

The long sleep is over.

For three thousand years I have patiently watched and waited. The Prophecies foretold the day when the sun would reach out and touch the earth—when my slumber would end, when my ancient weapon would breathe, when my dormant glory would blaze once more upon the planet and its people.

That day has arrived.

But there can be no triumph without a battle. Every civilization tells the same story. Good requires evil; redemption requires sin. The legends are as varied as are the civilizations that spawned them— yet each contains that same nugget of truth.

So I am not alone. The Chosen One awaits me. The flare opened the inner eyes of the Visionaries, those who can join the Chosen One to prevent my reign. But in order for them to defeat me, they must first make sense of their visions.

For you see, every vision is a piece of a puzzle, a puzzle that will eventually form a picture . . . a picture that I will shatter into a billion pieces and reshape in the image of my choosing.

I am prepared. My servants knew of this day. They made the necessary preparations to confuse the Visionaries—all in anticipation of that glorious time when the countdown ends and my ancient weapon ushers in the New Era.

My servants unleashed the plague that reduced the earth's population to a scattered horde of frightened adolescents. None of these children know how or why their elders and youngers perished.

And that was only the beginning.

My servants have descended upon the chaos. They will subvert the Prophecies in order to convert the masses into unknowing slaves. They will hunt down the Visionaries, one by one, until all are dead. They will eliminate the descendants of the Scribes so that none of the Visionaries will learn of the scroll. The hidden codes shall remain hidden. Terrible calamities and natural disasters will wreak havoc upon the earth. Even the Chosen One will be helpless against me.

I *will* triumph.

PART I:

July 1, 1999

Ticktock, ticktock, ticktock . . .

Ariel Collins frowned at the windup Mickey Mouse clock on her dresser.

Ticktock . . .

Maybe it was time to get rid of that thing. Yeah. The ticking was way too loud. It wasn't as if the time of day mattered, anyway. Morning, afternoon, night: That was about as precise as she needed to get. If it weren't for the clock, she wouldn't even know she was late. Today's blowout was supposed to start in the morning. So right now, all the clock did was remind her that she was still *here*, pacing around her room like an idiot—instead of *there*, partying at Old Pine Mall with several hundred of her closest friends.

I'm gonna look for five more minutes. Then I'm gonna bolt.

Her eyes scanned the room again. The place really was a pit, wasn't it?

No wonder she couldn't find anything. Every desk and dresser drawer was open, dripping clothes and underwear and yellowed magazines onto her purple shag carpet. Her bed hadn't been made in seven

5

months. Her closet looked as if it had been hit by a bomb. She laughed out loud. She'd thought she put that bottle somewhere *safe*—but there really wasn't any space in here that could fit that description.

Oh, well. There was no point in obsessing over one lousy bottle of booze. She just hated showing up at a party empty-handed. Supplying alcohol made a statement: *Look, people—the action can't start without me.* It was a way of drawing people to her, of letting them know that this was *her* turf, *her* scene. . . .

Then again, the booze wasn't even hers in the first place. It was Caleb's. She'd come home one night a couple of days ago and found a half-empty bottle of peppermint schnapps on her bed. *Peppermint schnapps.* Where on earth had he found something so random? She'd really have to ask him about that. If Caleb Walker had a secret stash of liquor somewhere, there was no way she would let him keep it to himself.

She grabbed her overcoat off the rug and wriggled into the soft sleeves. He must have snuck in here and taken the bottle back himself. She stepped out into the hall. He was probably embarrassed—

"Ow!"

Her foot struck something—*hard*—and she flailed wildly for a moment, then grabbed the hall banister to keep from face-planting on the floor.

What the hell?

It was Leslie's book bag. Ariel scowled. Why would Leslie leave it right near the top of the stairs? Ariel could have broken her neck. She bent down to pick it up . . . and hesitated.

A note was pinned to the zipper.

6

Dear Ariel,

I thought you might want this back. It is yours, after all. See you at the party.

Peace, Love, & X-Rated Nudity,

Leslie Arliss Irma Tisch

P.S. I know, I know. You hate my full name.

P.P.S. Check out the chick on page 38. If you had been a seventies porn star, this would have been you.

Am I right?

Ariel's annoyance vanished into the air like a puff of smoke. She snatched up the heavy bag. There was definitely a book in there. A *big* book. She yanked open the zipper. . . .

"Yes!"

She knew what it was even before she laid eyes on that cheesy, airbrushed cover.

Skintight: The Illustrated History of Erotic Film.

"Leslie, you are the *best!*" she shouted. Her words reverberated through the empty house. She tossed the bag aside and stared at the cheap, weather-beaten cover—clutching the book in both hands as if it were a holy relic. She couldn't believe it. After five months, five *long* months, it was finally back where it belonged.

Home.

She blinked several times. All right. She wasn't going to get moved to tears over a dirty little book that Dad had kept secret in the first place. It was just . . . the book seemed to symbolize so much. Not what was *in* it, of course. But when Ariel had lost it back in February, she'd lost a piece of her past, one of the few reminders of the way things were before the plague. Before every single adult on the planet melted, including her father.

It was so *perfect* that Leslie was the one who happened to stumble across it—totally by chance. Ariel shook her head. She'd hated Leslie for finding it at first . . . well, for that and a lot of other reasons. But after a while Ariel had forgotten that Leslie even *had* the book. What mattered was that Ariel had a best friend.

Uh-oh. Ariel rolled her eyes. *My brain is starting to remind me of a Hallmark card.*

She chuckled softly, flipping through the fuzzy, lewd photographs until she reached page thirty-eight. *Hey, what do you know?* This chick *did* sort of look like her. Well, except for the makeup. But they both had the same brownish blond hair, the same hazel eyes. And that necklace around this woman's neck looked a lot like the one Ariel wore: a big, clunky piece of metal that hung from a thin silver chain. Of course, Ariel doubted very highly that this woman had gotten *her* necklace from some freak who believed in the Chosen One—

The front door slammed.

"Ariel?"

"Hey, Caleb!" She shut the book and bounded

down the stairs. "Caleb, you'll never guess what Leslie just gave me back. . . ."

Her voice faded. She jerked to a stop in the front hall.

Whoa. Caleb looked terrible. He was covered in snow and shivering, wearing an oversize coat that made him look totally emaciated. White flakes melted into his stringy brown bangs and dripped down the side of his face. His skin was deathly pale, too—except for his ears and nose, which were bright red.

"It's freezing out there," he muttered, his teeth chattering. "It turned into a full-on blizzard."

Ariel swallowed. She didn't want to think about the snow. No. A freak blizzard in July didn't do much for any warm fuzzy feelings she might have about the future. Especially considering the planet had already pretty much gone berserk.

"Do you want me to light a fire?" she asked quickly. "I think there's some wood in the fireplace."

He shook his head, then stamped the snow off his sneakers. "Nah," he mumbled distractedly. "I'll be all right."

"You sure?"

He nodded. "Yeah. So . . . uh, what did Leslie bring back?" He peered at the book.

Ariel smiled and held it up for him to see. "What do you think?"

"Oh." His tone was flat. He blinked. "Neat."

Neat? Her eyes narrowed. That wasn't exactly the response she expected—not for a coffee-table-sized book of pornography. "Caleb, are you all right?"

"Fine." He glanced around the hall. "So, what are you up to?"

9

All right. *Something* was bothering him. She placed the book on the mantel. "If you wanna know the truth, I was looking for that bottle of peppermint schnapps you left in my room," she said.

He stiffened suddenly.

"Y-you, uh—you *found* that?" he stammered, staring at her.

"You left it on my pillow, remember?"

He tried to smile, but he looked ill. "Uh, yeah. I guess . . . I guess I did."

"What's wrong?" she asked. She flashed him a wry grin. "Are you worried I'm gonna think you have a drinking problem? Come on, Caleb. I knew you had a drinking problem *way* before I found that bottle."

She paused, waiting for him to laugh. He didn't.

"Did you . . . How did you know it was mine?" he asked.

"Process of elimination," she answered dryly. She shook her head. What was his problem? It wasn't *that* big a deal. She drank by herself, too, sometimes.

"What do you mean?" he asked.

"Two people sleep in my bed, and one of them is me. Being as *I* didn't leave it there, I figured it had to be the other person."

He didn't say anything. His face was blank.

"Caleb, what's the *matter* with you?" she demanded. "Are you stoned or something?"

"No, no—I mean, it's nothing, really," he mumbled awkwardly. He lowered his eyes. "So, uh . . . what are you up to, anyway?"

Ariel grimaced. "You just *asked* me that, remember?"

10

His brow grew furrowed. "Oh, yeah . . ."

"Look, Caleb, I don't know *what* you've been smoking—but I think you might need some more fresh air to clear your head."

She strode to the front door and threw it open. Icy wind blasted her face. She winced, squinting out into the street. *Jeez.* The snow swirled so heavily that she couldn't see more than ten feet in front of her, nothing but a tempest of white specks.

"I don't know," he murmured. "I was thinking we could just hang here."

For a moment Ariel stood in the doorway, cringing at the bitter cold. Maybe that wasn't such a bad idea. Old Pine Mall was a forty-five-minute walk—in *good* weather. It would probably take twice that long to get there now, if they didn't die of frostbite first. But still, the party had already started. She didn't want to miss anything juicy. No, they should definitely tough out the journey. The thought of being trapped in her house while everyone else in town was raging . . .

"What do you think?" he asked.

She glanced over her shoulder. "I kinda want to hit the mall, you know?"

"Now?" he cried.

"There's a big bash, remember? Leslie put it together."

"Do you actually think people are gonna *go?*" Caleb demanded. He waved his hand out at the snow. "Everybody's at home, Ariel. They're all—"

"How do *you* know?" she interrupted. She smiled, but her eyebrows were knit. "Did you knock on every single door in Babylon?"

11

He frowned. "No, but I was just outside freezing my butt off, and I didn't see *one* kid."

"No duh," she retorted. "That's because they're all at the mall."

He shook his head and slumped down on the staircase. "Whatever. If you want to go, go ahead. I'm gonna stay here." He glanced up at her. "You won't find anyone."

Ariel glared back at him. For some reason, she found she was getting angry. She *knew* the party was on. It was Leslie's idea. And once Leslie made a plan, it didn't take long for everyone else to jump on board. Besides, the lousy weather was probably more of an incentive for people to snuggle together in a nice, warm, cozy place. Caleb just didn't want to go out into the cold again. Since when had he become such a wimp?

"What?" he asked.

"Nothing," she mumbled. She turned away and hunched her shoulders, bracing herself for the storm. "I guess I'll see you later. You know where to find me."

"Wait, Ariel . . . come on."

She slammed the door behind her.

If he wants to act like a loser, fine, Ariel said to herself, marching clumsily through the snow on her front walk. She kept her head down. *It's not my problem.*

Within seconds her toes began to burn. Frost nipped at her ears. Maybe she should turn around and change into boots, find a hat. Nah. She'd be fine. As soon as she got to the mall, she'd take off her sneakers and socks and warm her feet by the bonfire. She squinted into the whiteness and tried to curl up her toes as she clomped down the street. No force of nature was going to stop *her* from getting a buzz on—

"Hey!" a boy's voice called behind her. "Wait up!"

Caleb? She couldn't tell . . . the voice sounded deeper. But who else would it be? She knew he'd come to his senses. She tried to suppress a smile as she stopped and turned around.

Her face fell.

It wasn't Caleb at all. Two dorky-looking guys stumbled toward her, bundled up in down jackets that went out of fashion when Ariel was about five years old. One was wearing cheap sunglasses. In a *blizzard.*

"Hey," the one in the glasses gasped. "Where are you going?"

Ariel chewed her lip and glanced impatiently in the opposite direction.

"The mall," she muttered.

"We're going there, too!" he called.

She tried to force a smile as they drew close. "Cool," she said dully. Great. Just what she needed. *Hey, Leslie, I didn't bring any booze—but I brought these two geeks! Whaddaya think?*

"We heard there was gonna be a . . ." He paused in midsentence.

"What?" Ariel asked.

His eyes widened, zeroing in on Ariel's chest.

"Uh, *excuse* me?" Ariel snapped. "What are you looking at?"

His mouth fell open.

She folded her arms in front of her. Not only were they geeks; they were perverts. Why was it that some guys were incapable of controlling their hormones? Her sick brother, Trevor, was exactly the same way. He always used to stare at the bust of Ariel's former best friend—that being one Jezebel Howe, the goth rocker who made Ariel want to barf for about a zillion different reasons. But there was no point in thinking about all *that*. No. She was angry enough. Maybe she should have brought *Skintight* with her to keep these boys entertained.

"Your—your necklace," the boy stuttered in a hollow voice. His breath started coming fast, forming a quick succession of little white clouds. "It's . . ."

"Take it off!" the other boy suddenly yelled.

Ariel jerked back. What the—

"Don't wear it!" The first boy thrust a shaky finger at it. "It belongs to the Demon!"

Oh, man. Ariel rolled her eyes. Now she got it. These kids were COFs: Chosen One freaks. Today really was her lucky day, wasn't it? First a fight with Caleb, now *this*.

"It's evil," the boy with the sunglasses croaked. "You have to take it off. You have to give it to the Chosen One when she gets here because mm-rmmph . . ." The rest of his jabbering was lost in an incomprehensible gurgle.

"How could it be evil?" Ariel demanded. "One of *you* psychos gave it to me!"

But neither boy answered.

The first fell to his knees in the snow.

14

He shook his head—and his face turned bright red. A black bubble appeared on his forehead, then exploded in a small sprinkle of blood.

The plague!

Ariel recoiled in horror. She squeezed her eyes shut. *Oh, God. Why?* She shook her head and clamped her hands over her face. Maybe only one of them was getting sick. Maybe the other one would be okay. . . .

But after a few moments, when she dared to take a peek, she already knew what she would see. She *knew* it. It always happened this way.

Both boys were gone.

All that remained were two puddles of steamy black glop, half covered with a pair of ugly down jackets.

"Julia? Are you sure you don't want me to get you something?"

The words drifted past Julia Morrison, lost in the cacophony of the overcrowded barn. She knew that the question was directed at *her*—but she was incapable of replying or even reacting. Her grief was like a heavy suit of armor that shielded her completely from the outside world. She could only stand still, staring at the mass of kids huddling together in their dirty white robes in a desperate effort to stay warm. Why did they even bother? Most of the heat had already seeped through the rotting, snow-covered wood walls.

"You have to eat something. You haven't eaten in days. It's really not healthy. You're so skinny. I'm starting to get worried. . . ."

Why doesn't she leave me alone? Julia wondered, shutting the voice from her mind. She shivered. She used to love the musical lilt of Linda's English accent, those mischievous blue eyes and blond curls. . . . Julia almost thought of her as a storybook character come to life.

17

Not anymore.

". . . the Healer has some soup in his house, okay?" Linda was saying. "I can go get it."

Julia remained silent.

"Okay, Julia—look." Linda seized her shoulders with both hands. "Sooner or later, you're going to have to accept the fact that George is dead. Nothing can bring him back. But it's been almost a week already. I don't mean to be cruel, but the plague is part of our lives now. You know that. And if George hadn't defied the Healer, maybe he could have been saved—"

"Go away!" The words exploded out of Julia's mouth. She quickly lowered her eyes. A veil of dark curls fell in front of her soft, brown face. *Watch it,* she warned herself. Outbursts like that were not smart. No, she had to keep her fear and anger and suspicion hidden. If Linda suspected that Julia was beginning to doubt their friendship, she might tell the Healer.

"I—I'm only trying to help," Linda murmured, swallowing. "I'm your friend."

No, you're not, Julia retorted silently. *You made George seem like a threat, so the Healer let him die. You destroyed the one love I've ever had and ever will.*

"I'm *more* than your friend, Julia," Linda stated in the silence. "I'm your partner. I'm a Visionary, like you. We share things. We know about the Chosen One, about the Demon. We feel the same pull to move west. We're *sisters.*"

Julia took a deep, shaky breath and met Linda's gaze. "You—you're right," she lied. "I'm just . . . I

18

need to be alone to deal with this, okay? Can't you understand that?"

Linda shook her head. "I understand. But I just don't think that being alone is a good idea." She glanced around the barn, then leaned forward, bringing her lips to Julia's ear. "I'm not only worried about *you*, you know. I'm worried about your baby. You need to eat—"

"Shhh!" Julia hissed. She edged away from Linda. "Don't *talk* about that! You swore you wouldn't tell anyone—not until I start showing!"

"I won't," Linda whispered anxiously. "But not talking about it isn't going to make it go away. You *have* to think about it. And you'll start showing soon. It's already been four months."

Julia's jaw tightened. Where did Linda get off, giving Julia advice about the well-being of her baby when Linda had all but killed the baby's father? Rage threatened to burst through Julia's blank facade once more, but she fought it back.

"Fine," she whispered after a moment. Her voice was strained. "Go get me some soup."

Linda hesitated. "It's not as simple as that—"

"What do you want me to say?" Julia cried. The heads of a few kids turned. *Uh-oh.* She bit her lip, struggling to keep her voice down. "I need time, all right?"

"I know, I know. But I think you need to start reaching out to people who will be willing to lend a hand. Like the Healer. Like Luke."

Luke? Julia's jaw dropped. For a moment she thought that Linda was playing some kind of sick joke.

19

"Look, I know what he did to you in the past," Linda went on, as if answering an unspoken accusation. "And nothing will ever change that. But he's *different* now, Julia. I've spoken to him. He can't sleep at night. It tears him apart to think about all the things he put you through—"

"You don't know anything about it!" Julia spat. Any last vestige of self-control disappeared. At least she could understand Linda's contempt for George; after all, George had tried to defy the Healer. But defending *Luke* . . . not only was that intolerable, it was disgusting. "Whatever he said to you was a lie, Linda. *I* know. *I'm* the one who went out with him. *I'm* the one who used to get beaten up. He's evil. He's barely even human."

Linda blinked a few times. "I . . . I . . . ," she sputtered.

Smack!

Julia flinched. *Good Lord—*

Somebody had slapped the back of her neck. *Hard.* She spun around, half expecting to see Luke's scarred, haggard face and raised hand.

But nobody was there.

"Julia?" Linda asked. "What's—"

Smack!

"Ouch!" Julia cried. There it was again. She whirled back around to face Linda. But Linda's hands were at her sides. Her forehead was tightly creased.

"What is it, Julia?" she asked.

"I—" The words stuck in Julia's throat.

All at once, her knees buckled. The barn floor seemed to accelerate suddenly, as if it had just been

20

hooked up to a jet engine. She couldn't keep her balance. She couldn't breathe. Her heart started hammering.

What's happening to me? she wondered frantically. She couldn't be slipping into a vision; this was far more powerful. Besides, she hadn't had any visions since the snow started. But her eyesight was fading. A creeping darkness enveloped her entire body. And she could feel that familiar sense of vertigo—only it was a thousand times stronger than before, sucking her down into a vortex of blackness. . . .

I'm scared.

I've never seen this place before. I think I'm in a room . . . but there are no walls, no ceiling overhead. There's a fire burning—a huge crackling blaze, shooting sparks and cinders into the air. A girl stands in front of it. Very near. I can't see her face. She's right next to the flames. . . .

"*I need help,*" *she says.*

I take a step forward. The heat is too great; I can't move any farther. I can only see the slender silhouette of the girl's body. How can she stand to be so close?

"*Who are you?*" *I ask.*

"*You know who I am.*"

I take a deep breath. I'm very frightened now. "*I want you to tell me,*" *I insist.*

"*You trust the Healer,*" *the girl says. She sighs and shakes her head.* "*Can't you smell the Demon's stench on him?*"

"*What are you saying?*"

"*You'll find out soon enough. You have to.*"

Tears flow down my cheeks. "I don't understand."

"Time is short, Julia. Time is very, very short. The Demon is stronger than you think."

I shake my head. And in the flickering light of the fire, I can see something else now: an hourglass . . . an old hourglass filled with black sand. It's very tall— taller than a person. It's standing right beside the girl. It's almost empty. The last of the blackness tumbles swiftly through the narrow funnel. . . .

"Remember what you've seen," the girl says. "Time is running out."

I watch as the final grain falls—

The hourglass explodes in flame.

I fall back, stricken. The girl is swept up in fire, burning from head to toe . . . completely consumed. But she doesn't move. Something is wrong. Something is terribly wrong—

Julia's eyes snapped open. She found herself staring up at falling snow—an endless stream of white flakes against the backdrop of a starless night sky. Her lungs heaved; sweat poured down her face. But she was *freezing*. Her body was soaked, trembling, in pain. . . .

"Are you awake?" a shaky voice whispered. "Can you hear me?"

Luke? She shook her head, utterly bewildered. Where was she? And what was *he* doing with her? Wasn't she in the barn a minute ago?

"Just take it easy," he murmured. "Don't try to sit up straight."

So she was lying down. Outside. *That* much she

could understand. She turned in the direction of Luke's voice. His face hovered above her own—that hideous, gaunt, scabbed mask. His blue eyes were puffy and red; his skin was wet with tears. He shook his head and brushed his stringy black hair behind his ears.

"What . . . happened?" she croaked.

He didn't answer. He simply crouched down in the snow beside her, sobbing.

"Luke?" A hot flash of panic shot up her spine. "Where am I?"

"You're with me," he choked out. "You're safe. Don't worry. You're safe. . . ."

**Old Pine Mall,
Babylon, Washington
4:30 P.M.**

My God. Where did they all come from?

Trevor Collins lay flat on his stomach, peering over the edge of the balcony at the food court several stories below. A sea of moving bodies stretched as far as he could see. Never in his wildest dreams had he imagined so many kids would be here. Their random perpetual motion reminded him of a videotape he had once seen in a high school biology class: a documentary about an insidious strain of swarming, multiplying bacteria.

"What is it?" Barney hissed from the shadows behind him. "Can you see anything?"

"Take a look," Trevor murmured. He licked his dry lips. Fear prickled at the back of his neck. He fought to ignore it. "See for yourself."

Barney slithered up beside him and shoved his pudgy face into the narrow space between the dusty marble floor and the base of the metal railing.

"God, Trev!" he gasped. "There must be, like, five hundred kids down there. We have to get out of—"

"Shut up!" Trevor whispered harshly. This was no time to panic. Besides, they were safely out of sight,

25

hidden away in the darkness. Only a few scattered bonfires on the first floor provided any light. A haze of smoke filled the air. Nobody could see them up here.

But Trevor could hear Barney's wheezing breath over the hollow roar of the distant voices, and it fueled his own anxiety. He felt as if he were watching an audience waiting for a punk rock concert—a drunken mob that was packed into a space far too small, poised on the verge of a riot. . . .

"I really think we should go," Barney whispered. "I'm serious."

"I didn't hike two hours through a blizzard just to turn around," Trevor muttered. "If you want to go back, fine. Personally, I think we're safer here."

"What are you *talking* about?" Barney demanded. "It doesn't—"

"Use your head, you idiot," Trevor interrupted angrily. "Most of the kids down there hate our guts. And they know that we know that. So the last place they'd expect to find us is right *here*, right next to them."

Barney chewed his flabby lip for a moment. "But what if they do find us? Huh? We can't protect ourselves."

"And you think we *can* back on campus?" Trevor shook his head. "We have two boxes of bullets left. The security system is shot. You've been talking about fixing it for two months, and you haven't done crap. Only ten of the TV monitors still work. Ten out of eighty. You really—"

"It's not my *fault!*" Barney cried. "The blizzard screwed everything up—"

26

"Shhh!" Trevor whispered. "Keep your voice down, or somebody *will* find us." He took a deep breath, trying to calm himself as he gazed down at the unruly rabble. "We didn't come here to argue. What's done is done. We came here to see how many kids there are, how organized they are, and what they plan to do. That's it."

Barney sighed. "Fine. Then we're finished. 'Cause as far as I can tell, they aren't organized at all. They're just here to get wasted. Look at those cases of beer and stuff over by the fountain. If they were organized enough to do anything to us, they would have done it a long time ago."

Trevor didn't answer. Barney was right, of course. Trevor often managed to forget that the fat imbecile was actually fairly perceptive.

But Trevor had come here for other reasons . . . not the least of which was to try to find Jezebel. He still had no idea how she'd managed to escape him. He'd locked her in the only secure spot left on the grounds of the Washington Institute of Technology—a windowless lab that he'd specially barricaded with the two-inch-thick steel door from the command center. He'd checked and double-checked the locks again and again. It didn't make any sense.

"You think your sister and her friend Leslie are down there?" Barney asked.

"Probably." Trevor sneered. "If there's free beer, Ariel's there. But to tell you the truth, I really don't give a crap. I hope I never see her again."

Barney glanced at him. "Then why'd you bother

locking her up in the first place? You spent all that time starving her and—"

"I thought she could help me," he snapped. "I thought she could shed some light on why the hell Jezebel was acting so weird. They *were* best friends, you know."

"Sorry," Barney mumbled. "Jeez. Chill out. I was just asking."

Trevor's jaw tightened. He suddenly felt agitated, out of sorts. Was he telling the truth right now? Or was he lying—to Barney and to himself?

He'd *had* to torture Ariel. He needed information. That was why he did it. Right?

Ariel deserves to be punished. The thought popped into his head before he could stop it. He shouldn't think things like that, not about his own sister. How many times had Dad told him that? How many times had he begged Trevor to forgive Ariel?

Trevor tried to swallow, but his mouth was too dry. Maybe Dad had been wrong. Maybe she *did* deserve it. He shouldn't feel any guilt. After all, he knew some things about Ariel. Ah, yes . . . he knew that she wasn't all she pretended to be. Beneath that carefree facade and phony charm lurked something poisonous—

"Trevor?"

"What?" he spat.

"Can we go now?"

Trevor rolled his eyes. "In a minute. I just want—"

"Hello, boys," a girl's voice interrupted.

Jeez! Trevor started—and his head slammed against the bottom of the railing. White light flashed in front of his eyes. Barney began to squirm beside

28

him, wriggling like a bloated fish caught out of water. With a violent shove Trevor pushed himself away from the edge of the balcony and rolled over on his back.

"Jezebel?" he gasped.

Her pale face glowed red in the dim light of the bonfires far below. It seemed to float in empty space, her hair invisible in the blackness behind her.

"Why do you keep calling me that?" she asked with a smile. "You know I'm not Jezebel anymore. I've *told* you that."

For a moment Trevor was unable to do anything but gape helplessly into her glittering, dark eyes. They looked like two wet stones. His heart pounded. His skull throbbed in pain. What was she doing up here? How the hell did she even *find* them?

Jezebel stepped over to the railing. "Quite a view, isn't it?" she murmured.

Finally Trevor managed to get enough control of himself to scramble to his feet. His wobbly legs almost gave out from under him, and he clutched the railing for support. Barney cowered on the floor, quivering uncontrollably.

"How did you know we were here?" Trevor whispered. "Did you see us?"

She shook her head. "Nope. It was a lucky guess. I figured some kids would have wandered away from the party." She cast him a sidelong glance. "I wasn't expecting *you* guys to show, though. Hanging out at a beer fest is so unlike you, Trev."

Trevor gulped. "We—well, we're leaving." His eyes flashed to Barney. *"Now."*

29

"Don't you want to talk?" she asked. "I mean, we haven't seen each other in a while. It's funny. I forgot how much you look like Ariel."

"Jez, listen—"

"And I *know* the reason you came here was to spy on me."

Trevor's insides seemed to turn to liquid. How did she do it? How did she know what he was thinking . . . all the time? She didn't used to be like this. No, something very disturbing had happened to her. And she was right: Whoever she was, she *wasn't* Jezebel. Trevor had never feared Jezebel Howe. He'd never feared anyone. Especially not a girl. But this person, this *thing* she had become, this was different.

"You probably want to know how I managed to escape," she remarked casually. "But that's not really important in the long run." She gestured to the crowd. "What's important is what's going on right here, right now."

"What are you talking about?" Trevor asked shakily.

Jezebel shook her head and laughed. "It's not what *I'm* talking about." She jerked her head toward the food court. "It's what *they're* talking about."

"But we can't hear anything from up here!" Barney cried from the floor. "We can't—"

"Barney, *please,*" Jezebel cut in. "Control yourself."

Trevor drew in his breath. "So what is it? What are they saying?"

"Well, you remember that girl Leslie? It turns out she's really . . . what's the word?" She snapped her fingers. "*Motivated*. Yeah, that's it."

30

Trevor's eyes narrowed. "I don't have time for games, Jez. I need—"

"Well, I *do* have time for games, Trevor dear," she interrupted. She looked him in the eye. "I have all the time in the world. What are you going to do, take me prisoner?"

Trevor blinked. His heart was beating so hard and fast that he was certain she could hear it.

"No." Jezebel snorted. "I didn't think so. Well, to make a long story short, most of the kids down there believe in the Chosen One. Most of them know that *you* tried all sorts of nasty experiments on kids who believe in the Chosen One. And Leslie's getting them all together so they can organize a huge attack on WIT. It's gonna happen at the end of the month. That's all."

The color drained from Trevor's face.

"Scared?" Jezebel taunted.

He shook his head. If Leslie were really organizing people, wouldn't this party look a lot more, well . . . *organized?*

"You don't believe me?" she murmured. "Go downstairs and see for yourself."

Trevor stared at her, scrutinizing her face for any trace of deceit, any hint she might be lying—but there was none. Was she telling the truth? In spite of all her sick behavior, Jezebel had never actually *lied* to him before. Then again, what motive did she have for warning him about something like this? Didn't she hate him?

"Look, Trev—I'm not out to get you or anything," she stated. "I just want to stop all the stupid fighting. It doesn't do anybody any good."

"I . . . I know," he muttered. "I don't get it, though. I mean, why would they even bother to attack me? Ariel already tried to attack me once, and Leslie knows what happened. She saw half her friends get mowed down."

Jezebel sighed. "Leslie isn't Ariel, Trev. She's more like those Chosen One kids—she doesn't drink or smoke or anything. She's really sharp, you know? People listen to her. And unfortunately, they're all pumped to kick your ass."

Damn. Trevor lowered his eyes. If this was true, then he was doomed. It was that simple. His worst paranoid nightmares would become a reality. There was no possible way he could defend himself against all those kids.

"Of course, if Leslie were out of the picture, things might be different," Jezebel said.

Trevor glanced up sharply—but before he could say anything, Barney stumbled to his feet and yanked him by the jacket collar.

"We're *out* of here," he snapped. He dragged Trevor roughly down the hall.

"Just think about it," Jezebel called after them. "*Ariel* sure as hell won't try anything. She's too busy getting plowed. Leslie's the only one who's together enough to organize anything." She flashed one last smile. "I'd get rid of her if I were you. . . ."

Her voice faded into silence as Barney shoved Trevor through a stairwell door.

"Easy!" Trevor barked. He scowled at Barney, smoothing his rumpled sleeves. "I know how to walk, for chrissakes. . . ."

But Barney was already bounding down the stairs.

"We're leaving, Trev," he yelled over the echo of his own clattering footsteps. "That's *it*. We should just get the hell out of town. It's too dangerous. We'll have a much better chance of finding a cure for the plague if we don't have to worry about all this crap. I don't want to be in the same *state* as Jezebel. Or Leslie. Or any of them. All right?"

Trevor shook his head. Leave? After all he'd accomplished? Just run away—proving that he was a coward to Jezebel, and Ariel, and Leslie, and every one of those stupid, drunken kids? Fat chance.

No, Jezebel was right. Without any kind of leadership, the kids in this town were incapable of doing anything but partying themselves to death.

"Come on!" Barney yelled. "That girl is a *freak*, man! Don't you get it? Something happened to her! She's got powers!"

Exactly, Trevor answered silently. *She's got powers. She can see things that we can't. So that's why we're going to take her advice. We're going to take care of Ariel's new best friend and stop this nonsense for good.*

CHAPTER FOUR

"Julia! Julia! Where are you?"

Dr. Harold Wurf was exhausted. His voice was growing hoarse. He took a deep breath and mustered one last shout.

"Julia!"

But the cry went unanswered, forming another icy cloud that was instantly swallowed up in the endless, driving snow.

"Julia?" Linda yelled beside him in the night. She swung a flashlight through a grotesque tangle of gnarled tree branches. "Julia . . . can you hear us?"

Harold groaned. It was hopeless. If he and Linda wandered this frozen wasteland any longer, they would suffer frostbite, maybe even hypothermia. Harold's extremities were already numb. He knew that his immune system was suffering. He was putting himself at risk for pneumonia. Tuberculosis as well. And he couldn't afford to get sick—not now, not when his flock needed him the most. The blizzard had decimated any remaining crops, destroyed his followers' morale . . . and in all likelihood already taken the life of Julia Morrison.

35

"What's the matter?" Linda asked, shouting to be heard over the wind.

"We've been out here for two hours," Harold yelled back. He shivered, then pulled his wool cap down tightly over his ears. *Ouch!* His scalp stung. His long dark hair was freezing solid at the roots. "We've covered almost every square inch of my property. I think we have to resign ourselves to the fact that we aren't going to find her—"

"But we *have* to!" Linda cried. "We can't lose her. She's a Visionary. You have to protect the lives of the Visionaries at any cost. It's your only hope for defeating the Demon. Your *only* hope. Don't you understand that?"

Harold paused, frowning. He glanced back through the woods toward his farmhouse. Right now, he wasn't overly concerned with the Demon. No. Right now, quite frankly, Linda's portentous warnings sounded like a lot of superstitious blather. Okay, fine: He knew he had an obligation to take the matter seriously; he *was* the Chosen One. But at this very moment all he wanted to do was settle into a nice hot bath. With a glass of wine. And Linda. His cracked lips twisted into a smile. Yes, yes. He still hadn't had a chance to see that tall, slender body of hers unclothed. She wouldn't mind warming up a little, would she?

"We have to keep looking," Linda pleaded. "Every vision is a link in a chain. I told you that. If we lose just one of those links . . . ."

"I thought you said you *stopped* having visions," Harold grumbled.

"I did," she replied. "We all did. But I know that

as soon as the snow clears and the final sign comes, our visions will return, as strong as ever. I *know* it. That's why it's so important—"

"Okay, okay," Harold interrupted. He shifted on his feet to keep his blood circulating. He wasn't any more thrilled about the prospect of losing Julia than *she* was. After all, Julia was beautiful . . . and available. Her little twerp of a boyfriend was dead—vanished in a puddle of black slime. But there was no point in considering the possibility of a romantic tryst with sweet Julia. She was gone. Both he and Linda simply had to accept that fact and move on with their lives.

"I'm just a little concerned about my health," he mumbled.

"*You?*" Linda cried. "But you're the Healer! You can stop the plague! You have the power over life and death!"

Harold sighed. Intellectually, he knew that was true. He'd cured people with just a touch of his hands. He *couldn't* get sick. Yet he certainly didn't feel as if he had any supernatural healing powers. He just felt cold, wet, and miserable. He almost laughed. Who would have imagined that his awesome abilities would work *against* him? Judging from the fierce determination on Linda's face, she was bent on keeping him out in this blizzard until she collapsed. After all, if she fell ill, he could heal her, right?

"Look, Linda, I appreciate the urgency of the situation. So if you want to keep looking, fine. But it's not my responsibility." His voice hardened. "It's yours. You were supposed to keep an eye on her. You were the one who let her go." Linda swallowed, shuddering with cold. "I know. I'm sorry. But I couldn't help it. I was in the barn, you know, talking to her, and—and she slipped into a trance. Or something. I don't even know. All I know is she just got up and ran off before I could even say any—"

"A *trance?*" Harold cut in.

"I think so." Linda shrugged.

His eyes narrowed. He'd never seen Linda so unsure of herself. She was by far the most confident and articulate member of his flock. She was the only one who even *approached* his level of intelligence. But now she sounded as lost and confused as everyone else. "You didn't mention that before," he said. "What do you mean?"

Linda lowered her gaze and shook her head. "I don't know."

"Do you mean she was having a vision?"

"Maybe." She bit her lip. "I don't know. That's why I didn't want to mention it. It was either a vision, or . . . or . . ." She didn't finish.

"Or *what?*" Harold pressed.

"Or the Demon has her under a spell or something."

The Demon. Every conversation always came back to the Demon. Harold scowled. Who *was* this damned Demon, anyway? And what was his relationship to Harold?

But that wasn't even the real question.

No. The real question was this: Why was Harold even faced with such a bizarre crisis? How had he

38

reached this point in his life—a point where he had to concern himself with a mysterious, nonhuman entity? When all was said and done, he was just a twenty-year-old medical student, for God's sake.

Well, that wasn't quite true. He was much more than that. But in all the months since January, when the first helpless kids started to believe he was a savior, he'd never stopped to reflect on what was truly happening to him or what people expected of him. He never had time. The events of his life simply *happened,* thundering along like an ever growing avalanche—unstoppable and incomprehensible, even to himself.

"Do you see why I'm so worried?" Linda asked quietly.

Harold nodded. "I guess. But I still—"

"Wait!" Linda interrupted. She held up a finger. "Listen!"

Harold held his breath. He strained his ears.

"Do you hear that?" Linda whispered.

Yes. Barely, just barely, hidden in the low murmur of the wind, Harold could hear a faint voice: *"Help . . . help me . . ."*

He frowned. So much for finding Julia. That was a *guy's* voice.

"That's Luke!" Linda cried.

In a flash she was dragging Harold through the woods, thrusting her flashlight out into the darkness. He nearly tumbled into the snow. Ice-laden branches lashed at his face and upper body. *Dammit.* What was going on? Who *cared* if it was Luke? Harold had already saved his life once. The fool needed to learn to take care of himself. . . .

"Help me!" the voice cried again. It was much closer now.

"Luke?" Linda yelled breathlessly.

"Over here!" Luke grunted. He sounded strained, as if he were struggling to lift a heavy object. There was a rustling noise. "Hurry! I can't hold on to her!"

Her?

Linda let go of Harold's hand and dashed forward. Harold kept his eyes pinned to the bouncing flashlight beam as Linda hurtled over a fallen tree trunk . . . and all at once, out of the black night, appeared two figures in white robes wrestling in the snow.

"Julia!" Linda shouted.

My God. Harold stopped short by the tree trunk. It *was* Julia. She was clawing her way across the ground, eyes closed, kicking at Luke. . . . He was on top of her, both arms wrapped around her waist, trying to tackle her. But he couldn't. Harold hadn't realized she was so strong for somebody so slight. It was unbelievable. She was completely out of control. For a moment Linda stood and pointed the flashlight at them, spotlighting them as if they were a circus act.

"Help me!" Luke barked. "I can't hang on!"

Linda glanced back at Harold. But before either of them could make a move, Julia abruptly stopped writhing—and collapsed into the snow under Luke's body.

She lay still.

"Oh, my God," Luke whispered. "Julia?"

"What's going on?" She groaned.

Harold hopped over the tree trunk and shoved Luke aside, then reached down and gently lifted Julia

40

from the snow. *Not good.* She was shivering violently; her lips were blue. He unzipped his thick parka and wrapped it around both of them.

"What's going on here?" he demanded. He glared at Luke. "What are you doing?"

Linda swung the light into Luke's face as he pushed himself to his feet.

"Trying to stop her," he croaked. In the sickly yellow light his scabbed skin looked almost fake, as if it were covered in makeup for a cheap Hollywood horror movie. He hugged himself for warmth. "I found her a couple of hours ago. I tried to get her to come back, but she wouldn't. Something's wrong with her. She keeps blacking out, then running away. . . ."

"You have to let me go," Julia whispered. She ducked away from Harold. "I can't stay here. I'm sorry. I have to go."

Harold shook his head. "What are you talking about? What's going on?"

"W-w-west," she stuttered through chattering teeth.

Linda stepped forward and tried to put her arm around Julia's shoulders. "But we talked about this, Julia. We can't go west yet. We have to fight the temptation—"

"No!" Julia wailed. "I *can't* fight it. Just let me go!"

Harold fidgeted with the parka zipper. What had gotten into her? She was usually so docile and compliant. Was Linda right? Did this have something to do with the Demon?

"Tell me *why* you have to go west," Harold murmured. "Can you do that?"

Julia stared at him. Her eyes were wide. She shook her head.

"Why not?" Harold asked.

"I just *can't*, okay?" She took a step back. Her gaze flitted from Linda to Luke, then back to Harold. "Please. Just let me go. I'm sorry. I can't stay here. You don't need me—"

"That's the Demon talking!" Linda shouted. "That's not you!" She glanced at Harold. "Julia *knows* we need her. She isn't herself. Don't listen—"

"Leave me alone!" Julia screamed.

She whirled around and bolted into the night.

But Luke kicked out his leg—sending her flying face first into the snow.

This is insane. Harold's pulse began to accelerate. He had to get everyone back to his house or the barn, someplace warm and dry where he could think. Clearly Julia was suffering from some kind of mental illness—

"Grab her!" Linda shouted.

Luke fell on top of Julia, planting his knee in the small of her back and snatching both of her hands. He yanked them up in the air.

A cry of pain escaped her lips.

"I'm sorry, Jules," Luke whispered. He shook his head again and again even as he tugged at her arms. "I'm so sorry. I don't want to hurt you anymore. I just don't want you to hurt yourself. I'm so sorry. . . ."

"Get *off* me!" she shrieked.

Linda crouched beside them and grabbed one of Julia's kicking legs. She shot a hard stare back at

42

Harold, blinking rapidly as she fought to keep Julia still. "What should we do?" she demanded.

Harold took a deep breath. "We should take her back to my house," he said as calmly as he could. "We need to ask her some questions. Alone. In a safe place. Behind locked doors, where she can't hurt herself or anyone else—"

"No, no," Julia sobbed. "Please. Don't . . ."

"In the cellar," Harold finished.

For the briefest instant Julia's eyes met his own. A chill shot through his body. Her pupils were dilated; the whites were visible. They were the eyes of a lunatic . . . or some caged animal. He turned away.

"You know what will happen if you take me back there?" she snarled at him. "We'll all die. All of us. Even *you*."

PART II:

July 2-17

CHAPTER FIVE

I can't go on, Sarah Levy said to herself. *I can't go on. . . .*

She'd been repeating the same phrase for several hours now, but it had long since lost any real meaning. The words simply provided a monotonous accompaniment to the crunch of her feet through the snow. Left, right, left, right: I-*can't*-go-on; I-*can't*-go-on. . . . She felt like a doomed soldier marching blindly toward some far-off battle, forced to keep pace with a drummer in her own head.

"You think somebody will drive by anytime soon?" Aviva asked. "I don't even know if we're on the highway anymore."

Sarah lifted her gaze. Not on the highway? But . . .

My God. The landscape was flat. Her face had been tucked away in the folds of her coat, hidden from the wind; she hadn't even noticed. She just kept putting one foot in front of the other. But she and Aviva were stuck out in the middle of nowhere. *Nowhere.* A level plain of white powder stretched off in every direction, like a frozen ocean on some alien planet. There was no sign of a road, no sign of a town, no sign of anything—not even a telephone pole. She gaped at Aviva.

"See what I mean?" the girl grumbled. Her voice was muffled under a scarf wrapped tightly around her head. She looked like a Bedouin nomad, bundled up in blankets and sweaters—with a huge backpack that was stuffed with their paltry belongings. Sarah could see nothing of Aviva's body but her blue eyes, bloodshot and smarting from the cold. A few stray tufts of curly red hair hung over her shoulders.

"I can't get my bearings," Aviva said. "Can you?"

"I . . . I . . . ," Sarah stammered. Of course she couldn't get her bearings. They were lost. Why hadn't Aviva said something earlier? Hadn't she been paying attention? *Stupid, stupid, stupid.* The sky was already beginning to darken. The day would be over soon. And they wouldn't survive out in this weather overnight. Sarah whirled around and squinted at the parallel lines of their footsteps, fading quickly in the onslaught of snow.

"I guess we should just keep going," Aviva muttered.

Sarah shook her head violently. Waves of panic spread through her body. Her breath came so hard and fast that her glasses began to fog. "No way. We have to follow our tracks back to that motel where we slept last night. If we get stuck out here—"

"We *can't* turn around," Aviva interrupted.

Sarah glared at her. "Why not? Don't you get it? We'll die if we don't."

Aviva blinked, then glanced back at their tracks. "It would take too long," she stated quietly. "We've already been walking for six hours today. We have to keep moving."

"Even if it *kills* us?" Sarah cried. "You just said yourself that we're lost!"

"But we're headed in the right direction," Aviva countered. "We're headed south. We're getting close to Texas, right? We know that the False Prophet is in Texas."

Sarah hesitated. *Did* they know that the False Prophet was in Texas? Not really. They were just acting on a hunch . . . a hunch provided by two druggies in Pennsylvania who told them about some guy who claimed to be able to cure the plague. For all they knew, this guy had nothing to do with the False Prophet. And even if he did, there was a possibility that he wasn't even there anymore. Maybe he'd picked up and left. Maybe they were wasting their time. Maybe they were making a terrible mistake.

"I don't know," she finally murmured. "Maybe we should just turn around and think things over. It might make more sense to go west. Didn't you tell me you felt a weird pull out west?"

Aviva didn't answer.

Without warning, she pitched forward—slamming into the snow at Sarah's feet.

"Aviva!" Sarah cried. She fell beside the limp body and shook it. There was no response. Her heart raced.

"Aviva!" she yelled again. She held her breath. *God, no.* This couldn't be happening. Aviva couldn't just keel over for no apparent reason. Impossible. She was all Sarah had left. Everybody else had died or disappeared: her parents, her brother, her followers . . . Ibrahim, the boy whom Sarah had loved. But Aviva couldn't go the way of Ibrahim. No, no, no. She couldn't vaporize. She was the only one still alive who knew the truth—that Sarah was the Chosen One, that Sarah had somehow been picked to save the survivors of the plague from the demon Lilith. . . .

Aviva moaned.

That's good! With a grunt Sarah dug her fingers underneath Aviva's stomach and flipped her over on top of her backpack. Aviva's head lolled from side to side. Her eyelids began to flutter. Okay, that probably wasn't a good sign, but at least it meant she was alive.

"False Prophet," Aviva croaked.

Sarah cradled Aviva's upper body in her numb, red hands. "What?" she said shakily. "Come on. Wake up. Please, wake up—"

"Have to get to him soon," she whispered. Her eyes squeezed tightly shut. She began to shiver. "Time is running out. Have to get to him soon . . . or there won't be any hope for the Chosen One. . . . Have to stop him. Time running out . . ."

"Stop him from *what?*" Sarah whimpered. "Come *on,* wake up. . . ."

Aviva's eyes flew open.

"Aviva?" Sarah cried. "Aviva? Can you hear me?"

"What's going on?" The question was barely a whisper. She glanced to her left and right. "Why am I on the ground?"

"You passed out," Sarah said breathlessly. Warm

50

relief coursed through her veins, shutting out the cold. Aviva was fine; she was lucid. *Thank God.* "You were talking about the False Prophet. Do you remember what happened?"

Aviva nodded. "I think . . . I think I had a vision," she said. She sat up straight. All at once, she began to nod. "I *did* have a vision."

"What was it?"

Aviva frowned for a moment and stared off into space. "I saw the Demon," she said distractedly. "Yeah . . . I did. I saw Lilith. She's using the False Prophet. She's going to lead him away. We have to get there soon, though. Like *now.*" She started pushing herself off the ground, grunting under the strain of the backpack.

Sarah shook her head in bewilderment. "But why? I don't understand—"

"Time is running out," Aviva muttered. She straightened and wobbled for a moment, then dusted the snow off her arms and legs. "It's . . . it's not good."

"Well, can you explain it to me?" Sarah demanded impatiently. She hopped to her feet. "Why is there such a rush?"

Aviva gazed at her. "The False Prophet is about to leave. He's going to go west." Her voice was cold, almost unrecognizable. "If you don't get there in time to stop him . . ." She left the sentence hanging.

"But how do you *know* all this?" Sarah cried.

"Because I saw the scroll in my vision, too," Aviva stated.

The scroll! A pang of longing shot through

Sarah's body. Her granduncle's ancient parchment was lost forever, lying at the bottom of New York Harbor. She shook her head. She should have tried harder to save it. She should have risked her life when she had the chance. She *knew* the scroll was blessed with magical properties; it couldn't be destroyed. And those mysterious prophecies contained the only key to defeating the Demon. As long as they remained hidden from her, she would grope blindly toward a destiny she didn't even understand.

Unless . . .

Wait a second. Aviva is Israeli. The scroll is written in Hebrew.

"How much did you see?" she asked excitedly. "I mean, could you read it?"

Aviva nodded slowly. "I think so," she mumbled. "Yeah . . . I think I could."

Sarah gasped. "What did it say?"

"It said . . ." Aviva hesitated, narrowing her eyes. "It said that the False Prophet is going to be led astray by the servants of the Demon." She held her breath, then sighed apologetically. "I'm sorry. That's all I can remember."

"Do you know what will happen when he leaves?"

Aviva shook her head. "All I know is that we have to stop him. We—" She abruptly broke off, craning her neck to peer at something over Sarah's shoulder. "Oh, my God!" she cried. A huge smile broke out on her face. "Sarah, look! A car!"

Sarah spun around.

Sure enough, a pair of headlights was bearing

down on them through the snowfall like the glowing eyes of some fantastic creature. . . .

"Hey!" Aviva shouted. She stumbled forward and planted herself directly in the path of the beams, then began jumping up and down, waving her arms maniacally. "Hey! Slow down! Hey! Help us! Help!"

It always happens. Sarah's mouth hung slack in amazement. *Just when things can't get any worse, a miracle saves me.*

She could see now that the headlights belonged to an old minivan: a rusted, dented heap of junk with tinted windows that looked as if it was at least ten years old. It slowed and stopped. The engine puttered loudly.

"Hey!" Aviva yelled again.

After a moment the driver's side window lowered with a soft buzz. A scruffy-looking teenage boy poked his head out and cocked his eyebrow at her.

"Are you okay?" he asked.

"We are now," Aviva choked out. All of a sudden she burst into tears. "Thank *God* you found us. Thank *God* . . ."

The boy glanced at Sarah. "What are you-all doing out here?"

Sarah shrugged. "We're lost," she said simply. What else could she say? *Hi. I'm the Chosen One. But I don't have my magic scroll. So my friend and I have been wandering the country in search of the False Prophet so we can find the Demon. . . .* Yeah, right. The guy would probably gun his engine and run her over.

"You want a ride?" he asked, glancing between the two of them.

"That would be great," Sarah answered tentatively. "Uh . . . where are you going?"

The boy looked at her as if she were insane.

"I'm going to the Promised Land. I'm going to be *saved*. Come on, hop in." He slapped the door with his palm. "There's plenty of room. It's just me and my friend Paul. We can all meet him together."

Sarah frowned. "Meet . . . who?"

"Who?" He laughed once. "Who do you *think?* The Chosen One."

**Old Pine Mall,
Babylon, Washington
Night of July 4**

Caleb Walker always looked forward to the Fourth of July. Yes, sir. The holiday made him proud to be an American. He loved everything about it: the fireworks, the cookouts, the Pledge of Allegiance, Mom, apple pie . . . the whole bit. And the beer, of course. Independence Day always provided a variety of beer-drinking opportunities. Sometimes the beer would come in kegs. Other times it would come in bottles. And so on.

As a matter of fact, the very first time he'd ever gotten drunk was on Independence Day. It was at his uncle Stan's house, five years ago. He was thirteen. He drank three cans of Schmidt's. He felt great. Then he went around to all the guests and finished what was left of *their* beers. Then he puked. It was awesome.

So why did *this* Fourth of July have to suck?

It should have been the best ever. He was *free:* free from school, free from relatives, free from a lame summer job. But the day was almost over, and he wasn't even wasted yet. He'd spent most of it alone in the snow. And now he found himself loitering in

55

some sorry suburban mall—in a dark, ice-cold, sludge-covered hall, no less—outside a huge party where his girlfriend was raging her butt off, conveniently forgetting that he even existed.

Okay. Whatever. He wasn't going to feel sorry for himself. This Fourth would have sucked, anyway, right? There couldn't be any fireworks or cookouts because of the damned blizzard. There couldn't be any Pledge of Allegiance because there was no real USA anymore. And there sure as hell couldn't be any Mom or apple pie because Mom had probably turned into a puddle of black sludge.

That left beer.

Mmmm. Sweet, frothy beer. All right. Time for some action. This was his plan: He'd march into the food court, head straight for the stacked cases of Budweiser, grab one, then come back out. And if Ariel saw him or tried to talk to him, he'd ignore her. He'd let her know how it felt. She could stay in that stupid food court for the next three years for all he cared. He wasn't going to be played like a chump. No way—

The door at the end of the hall opened.

The volume of the party swelled, as if somebody had turned up a TV. Caleb caught a brief glimpse of a smoky bonfire and some dancing bodies. The door closed.

A girl in a long black dress strode toward him.

Jezebel?

His shoulders sagged. Yup. Even before he could see her face, he knew. Nobody else styled their hair in that Medusa-like explosion. He shook his head. Why the hell had he even *come* here? He should have just stayed at Ariel's house and gone to bed.

"Caleb!" Jezebel called. She leaned forward and squinted toward him in the shadows, then picked up her pace. "Hey! Is that you?"

No, it's RuPaul.

"Man, I am so glad I found you!" she cried. She lurched to a halt in front of him. Her pale face was rosy. She clutched a familiar-looking bottle in one hand. It was peppermint schnapps. His stomach twisted.

"What's going on?" she asked. "Where have you been?"

"Uh . . . just wandering around," he mumbled. He caught a whiff of that sickly sweet mint odor and took a step back. "I wasn't even really planning on coming. . . ."

"I know what you mean," she muttered. She cast a disdainful glance over her shoulder. "That party totally blows. It's mostly Chosen One freaks. They were just singing the national anthem. Isn't that, like, the lamest thing you've ever heard?"

He shrugged. "It's the Fourth of July."

"Oh, right." She snickered. "Like that really *means* anything."

Caleb hung his head. After only ten seconds of conversation with this chick, he felt like running away. Either that or stuffing a sock down her throat. What had he been *thinking* the other night? Sure, she was kind of hot. Kind of. And she could be funny . . . as long as the person talking to her had already imbibed some powerful booze.

57

Unfortunately, he hadn't.

"I think I'm gonna go back to Ariel's," he muttered. "I'll see you later—"

"Why the rush?" she interrupted. Her voice was husky. She swished the bottle under his nose. For a moment he thought he might vomit on her. "You just got here. Don't you want a drink? Come on. I know you like this stuff."

"I *don't,* actually," he snapped. He lifted his eyes. "You know, Ariel found the bottle you left in her room the other night."

Jezebel laughed. "So what?"

"How many people do you think drink peppermint schnapps?" he demanded. "If she saw you drinking that, she might figure out that *you* were in her room, too. She might make the connection that we were together."

"Oh, *come on.*" Jezebel groaned. "Ariel's not that smart. Besides, she barely even noticed me." She took a sip from the bottle. "She's way too wrapped up in Leslie, you know?"

Yeah, Caleb thought dismally. *I do.*

What was with those two, anyway? They were always together. And Ariel used to hate Leslie. Back when Caleb and Leslie were fooling around, Ariel couldn't even stand to be in the same room as her. Now she wouldn't leave Leslie alone. Maybe they were falling in love or something. Yeah. *That* would be funny, wouldn't it? Maybe it was his fault. After all, he was the last one to fool around with either of them—at least as far as he knew. He had probably soured them both on the male half of the species. . . .

"Just hang out for a little, Caleb," Jezebel murmured. "Have a drink."

Caleb frowned at her. His eyes wandered down to the bottle in her hands. He'd rather drink old toilet water than take a sip of that stuff. Then again, beggars couldn't be choosers. He never got tired of that cliché. Without a word, he plucked the bottle from her grasp and upended it—then drained the rest of its bitter contents in a rapid series of gulps.

"Jeez, Caleb!" she cried, giggling. "Chill out!"

"Ahhhh," he breathed. He wiped his mouth on his sleeve. For a moment he teetered on the balls of his feet, slightly woozy. His throat burned. His stomach felt as if it had suddenly been filled with liquid concrete.

"Thanks a lot," she mumbled sarcastically.

He shrugged and handed her the empty bottle. Then he burped.

"Caleb!" she cried, wrinkling her nose. She sounded mechanical and phony, like a windup doll. "That is so gross. Aren't you at least gonna say 'excuse me'?"

"I hadn't planned on it."

She giggled again. "You're a real Prince Charming, you know that?"

"What can I say?" He grinned at her. "I was a frog in a former life."

Her smile widened. All at once, she burst into laughter.

Much to his surprise, he did, too. He couldn't help himself. It wasn't that funny . . . but for some reason, the world seemed like a much more funny place in general. He glanced around the filthy, dark hallway.

Even this dump wasn't so bad. A delicious sensation of warmth and contentment oozed through his body.

"Well, it's a good thing I brought my whole stash with me," Jezebel stated once she managed to get a grip on herself. She carelessly tossed the bottle over her shoulder. It shattered on the floor. Caleb winced. She grabbed his hand. "Come on. I hid three more bottles in the toy store—"

"Whoa, whoa," Caleb protested. "I gotta talk to Ariel."

"Why?" She rolled her eyes and tugged at his arm. "What are you gonna say to her?"

Caleb hesitated. That was a very good question, actually. What *was* he going to say to her? He certainly wasn't going to apologize for that fight three days ago. That was her fault. It was too cold to go to the mall. Well, he supposed he did end up coming to the mall, anyway. But he didn't enjoy the two-hour trek through the snow. No . . . *she* was the one who owed *him* an apology. Not the other way around. Right. If there was any talking to be done, she would have to initiate it.

"Come *on*." Jezebel moaned—and the next thing he knew, she was whisking him down a side corridor and through a pair of open double glass doors . . . into what looked like some kind of voodoo temple.

A smile spread across Caleb's face. So this was where Jezebel liked to keep her booze. No wonder. The place had her name all over it. Burning candles lined the shelves, casting an eerie glow over rows and rows of hideous masks and action figures. Their dusty, smiling faces seemed to leer at him. The whole vibe was really freaky—but in a childlike, Hollywood kind of way.

"Check out these fun-house mirrors," Jezebel insisted, dragging him quickly to the back of the store.

"I . . . I . . . ," he stammered. He wanted to slow down for a second, but he couldn't seem to transform his thoughts into words. A pleasant fog settled over his brain. He felt numb and disassociated from the outside world—as if he were watching a video instead of *experiencing* life.

Jezebel rounded a corner and stopped in front of a pair of enormous, curved pieces of glass. *Wow.* He hadn't seen anything like this since he was a kid, when his mother had taken him to a circus. . . .

"Aren't these great?" Jezebel asked.

Caleb grinned at his distorted reflection. It *was* pretty cool. He looked like a very fat dwarf. Except for his head, of course. That was about five feet tall. It was kind of nice to stare into a mirror and not feel self-conscious in any way. He didn't have to worry about how skinny he was, or how dirty he looked, or—

"These remind me of Ariel," Jezebel suddenly announced.

Ariel? Caleb glanced at her, caught off guard. "What do you mean?"

She shrugged. "Well, with these mirrors, you think you're looking at one thing, but you're really looking at another. The image is fake. What you see is definitely *not* what you get. You know what I'm saying?"

"No." Caleb's stare hardened. He didn't like the sound of this at all. "Explain it to me."

She turned to him. "Can I ask you something, Caleb?"

"Like what?"

Jezebel raised her eyebrows. "Have you noticed anything *weird* about Ariel lately?" Her tone was flat. "I mean, aside from the fact that she's got a crush on Leslie?"

He blinked. "What are you talking about?"

"I'm talking about the way people just happen to vaporize whenever she comes near them."

"What?" His face wrinkled in disgust. "That's . . . that's not even funny. It's *sick*. It's total bull, too. There's—"

"Is it?" she interrupted. "You know what I'm talking about, though. Don't you?"

Caleb glared at her. He opened his mouth . . . but his lips closed, as if he had no control over them.

He did know what she was talking about.

Three days ago, when they'd gotten into that fight, he'd watched her from the living room window as she stormed off. And he saw these two guys come up to her, and they . . . but no. That was just a coincidence. He swallowed. It *had* to be.

"See?" she muttered, as if he had answered out loud. She bent down behind the mirror and pulled out a fresh bottle of peppermint schnapps. "You *do* know."

"I didn't say that," he growled.

She shrugged, then unscrewed the cap and dropped it on the floor. "There's nothing so powerful as the unspoken." She took a sip and smiled. "My English teacher told me that. I think he was a drunk, too."

"Okay, fine," Caleb spat. "Let's say that it *is* true. Let's say people melt when they come up to Ariel." He snatched the bottle from her hands and chugged fiercely from it for a few seconds, spilling a few drops on his chin. "How do you explain it?"

"I can't," she murmured. "But I know a few things about Ariel that you don't. Things you can't even imagine. Things that I don't think she even knows herself."

Caleb sneered. What kind of pseudopsychological BS was *that?* But he couldn't think of anything to say. He took another slug.

"I'm serious." Her dark gray eyes bored into his own.

"You know what, Jezebel?" he snapped. "I really don't care. If you ask me, you sound like one of those Chosen One freaks. I don't want to *hear* it, okay?"

She took a step forward and placed her hand on his shoulder. "I just don't want to see you get hurt." Her tone softened. She began to massage his neck, very gently. "You're such a great guy. . . ."

He bristled. "Don't do that."

"Why not?" she whispered. She ran her other hand down his chest, gently scratching his shirt with her black fingernails. "What's the matter?"

A shivery tingle shot through his bones. He tried to step back, but his legs seemed to have turned to putty. Blood pounded to his head, clouding his thoughts. He knew he shouldn't be getting excited, but he couldn't help it. This girl was bad news. He didn't like her. Right? He *didn't*.

"That . . . that night in Ariel's room was a onetime

thing," he croaked. "I was just a little messed up. We can't do it again. Really. We can't—"

"Says who?" Jezebel asked.

He shook his head. "I . . ."

She pulled his head down and kissed him.

And as much as he hated himself for it, he didn't try to resist her.

Not even a little.

He kissed her back—softly at first, then more powerfully . . . then with a frenzy.

Within seconds they were rolling around on the floor, slipping out of their clothes. But he couldn't stop. All he wanted was to forget about where he was, about who he was, about *everything*.

Especially Ariel.

SEVEN

**Babylon,
Washington
July 5–10**

July 5

Things are starting to get really, really weird. I know I promised I was going to be Miz Positivity from now on, but I don't see it happening. I almost feel like running away. Or worse.

Last night was another nightmare. In fact, every single day of my life is like an awful sequel in a series of bad horror movies. The <u>Insanity</u> <u>of</u> <u>Ariel</u> <u>Collins</u>, <u>Part</u> <u>VIII</u>: <u>The</u> <u>Revenge</u> <u>of</u> <u>the</u> <u>Chosen</u> <u>One</u>.

I wish I could laugh, but it's not funny.

Anyway, it happened again. It was the third time in less than two weeks. I was wandering around the mall, looking for Caleb. Leslie said she thought she saw him around. But I ended up bumping into three COIs. They looked at me like they <u>hated</u> me. I've never seen a person's eyes look like that, like they were totally empty, like there was nothing behind them at all. Even Trevor's eyes have a spark of something.

I was frightened. I admit it. I said something like, "Hey, what's up?" I was trying to be nice for once, to make conversation. But two of them grabbed me by the arms. They held me so tight that it hurt. The third one tried to rip my necklace off. But before I could even scream, all three of them melted. At the <u>same time</u>. I'll never forget the feeling on my arms when it happened. It was like somebody spilled a plate of warm stew on me, with that black slime dripping on my clothes where their fingers had been. I don't think I've ever cried harder.

And I never did find Caleb.

July 6

Today Leslie admitted that she's really freaked, too. I don't know if that makes me feel better or worse. She's starting to think there might be something to what the COFs believe. She asked me: What are the chances that so many different kids from different places would end up being crazy in the exact same way? Why would they all end up in the same place?

I didn't have an answer. The truth is, I don't know <u>what</u> to think anymore.

What's happening to me? I can't do anything. I can't even <u>move.</u> I feel like there's a big heaviness in my head. It's like a thick, invisible curtain that separates me from the rest of the world, and no matter how hard I try, I can't get past it. I don't want to talk to anyone except Leslie. And I'm the one who couldn't stand to be alone. I'm the one who loved to party with as many people as possible, all the time.

But to be honest, I'm worried that if I talk to someone, they might end up melting.

I didn't say that to Leslie. I think she got the picture, though. She's been so awesome. She actually <u>listens,</u> unlike Jezebel, who just liked to hear herself talk on those few rare occasions I tried to share something serious with her. I feel like I can talk to Leslie about <u>anything.</u> Well, almost anything . . .

There's one thing I've kept to myself. It's this weird nervousness I feel all the time. And it's not just because I'm scared about the COTs. There's something else going on. It's like . . . I don't know. I can't really even write it down or articulate it. It pisses me off, too. Usually I'm good with words. The closest I can come to explaining it is that I have a feeling something bad is going to happen really soon. Something besides how I'm going to become a puddle of black glop when I turn twenty-one. Whatever this is, it's going to happen a lot sooner.

July 8

Ugh. I swear to God, I could <u>kill</u> Jezebel.

Why can't she just leave us alone? Today she comes barging into my living room, totally uninvited, ranting and raving about how Leslie should get all the COTs together and go kick Trevor's butt. Leslie and I just looked at each other. We haven't even talked about Trevor in, like, ages. Worrying about him is just a stupid waste of time. He can't hurt people anymore because everyone got out of WTS. (Including Jez, I might add.) That's all that matters. I really don't care _what_ he does. Leslie doesn't, either.

But Jezebel was all like: "Don't you care about how he tortured you? Don't you care about how he killed all those kids?" And I was like, "If it bothered you so much, how come you kept living with him? How come you _slept_ with him?"

In the end, Leslie had to physically throw her out of the house. It was kind of funny. Jez landed on her butt in the snow. Right when she got up, we slammed the door in her face. Then we started cracking up. It was the first time I actually laughed in about three weeks.

July 9

You know what I really miss about the old world? Advice columns. Or better yet, those phone-in talk shows like <u>Loveline.</u> I used to love listening to anonymous couples talk about their problems, like why somebody's boyfriend wouldn't have sex unless there was a sock puppet involved. When I was dating Brian Landau (RIP), I needed to hear stuff like that on a pretty regular basis in order to feel better about what was going on with us. It made us seem so <u>normal</u> in comparison.

Maybe that's why I have this really

depressing hunch that Caleb and I are doomed. There's nobody around to make us feel normal. Except the COYs, of course. But even though they're weird, none of them have problems with relationships. I don't think any of them are even interested in dating. What's the word for people like that? <u>Asexual?</u>

Anyway, today Caleb talked to me for the first time in, like, a week. I haven't even <u>seen</u> him in Lord knows how long. I guess I've kept a pretty low profile, but still, I've been at home. He knows where to find me. He used to <u>live</u> in my room, for God's sake.

But now he's crashing at the mall. He says he didn't feel like coming to see me until today because of the snow. Pretty lame excuse, if you ask me. But Caleb's sensitivity to bad weather was what started this whole fight in the first place, right?

Okay, maybe that's not fair. I know that some of the blame falls on me, too. I even apologized for being a bitch. I <u>never</u> apologize.

He didn't seem to care, though. He acted really nervous and skittish the whole time, like he couldn't wait to leave. And he was really rude to Leslie He told her to get lost, that he wanted to have a private conversation. "Can I just separate you two lovebirds for thirty seconds? I promise I won't touch Ariel." That's what he said, as if he was jealous of her or something. He must be hitting that peppermint schnapps a little too hard. How did things even get this bad?

Leslie had another run-in with Jez. I've never seen her so shaken up. Apparently Jez threatened her or something. She said that if Leslie didn't do something about Trevor, she'd regret it. It doesn't make any sense. If Jez is so hung up on Trevor, why doesn't she just do something herself? But nothing Jez does ever makes any sense.

That wasn't all that was bothering Leslie, though.

She also had a run-in with a couple of the COFs.

They say they hate me. They say that my necklace belongs to the Demon. They also say that the Demon is here, in Babylon, possessing somebody's body. It's obvious what they think. They think it's me. I told Leslie I wanted to just throw the necklace away. Maybe the necklace has something to do with why people suddenly seem to catch the plague whenever they come near me. I don't know. Nothing sounds too crazy anymore.

But Leslie told me to hold on to it. She said that as long as I have it, we know that it's safe. We know the Demon can't get to it. She actually _said_ that. Leslie Tisch. The girl who doesn't believe in anything. She was serious, too.

I'm so scared. I've never been more scared in my life, not even when Dad melted right in front of me. And it's not because Leslie is starting to believe in all this stuff about the Chosen One and the Demon.

It's because I'm starting to believe in it, too.

**Pawnee,
Oklahoma
Morning of July 11**

"So how much longer do you think it'll take us to reach this so-called Promised Land?" Sarah asked from the backseat of the minivan.

Neither boy in front answered.

"Another ten days? Another ten *years?*"

The boys glanced at each other. But they didn't say a word. They didn't even shrug.

Sarah's eyes smoldered. *Go ahead, just keep ignoring me,* she thought. *Just see what happens when I stop being polite.* All she needed was one last little *tap,* a microscopic *shove* over the edge. . . . She deserved a medal for self-control. She'd left most of her patience somewhere back in Missouri. What was the matter with these jerks? They seemed so nice and normal at first. Even their names reeked of normality. Paul and Jake. She assumed they were just a couple of regular guys. A little spaced-out and scraggly, maybe, but still regular.

But sometime on the first day, their behavior abruptly changed—without warning. It wasn't as if she or Aviva had done or said anything rude, either. No, in fact, they'd been overly grateful. Then bang:

77

Paul and Jake started giving them the silent treatment. Just like that. They literally stopped talking.

And they kept giving each other weird looks. What was *that* about?

So now the four of them slogged through the snow in silence, day after day, listening to the same warbly tapes over and over again on the crappy stereo. If Sarah heard another one of those whiny heavy metal ballads again, she'd scream.

Maybe it's time for Aviva and me to tell them the truth. Maybe they need a shock to wake them up. Sarah nodded to herself. Neither she nor Aviva had breathed a word about Sarah being the *real* Chosen One—or even about Aviva being a Visionary. Sarah wanted to scope out this other so-called Chosen One before she made any moves. And Aviva agreed that silence was the best policy. She didn't want to say anything that could possibly jeopardize their reaching this Promised Land as fast as possible. On the other hand . . .

"We'll be there tomorrow," Jake suddenly stated.

"What?" Sarah asked.

"If we just stop at night, we'll probably get to the Promised Land tomorrow," he said. "It's a good thing, too. We're almost out of food."

Sarah glared at the back of his head. There was a sour edge to his remark, as if he was somehow implying that it was *her* fault that they had run out of supplies.

"Well, I guess you shouldn't have picked us up in the first place," Sarah snapped.

Aviva nudged her and shook her head, wide-eyed. "Don't," she mouthed silently.

78

But if either Paul or Jake was upset, they didn't show it. They just kept staring through the flipping windshield wipers at the oncoming snow.

"What's the matter?" Paul finally asked. His voice was colorless.

"I just want to know why you guys decided to become mutes," Sarah answered.

He lifted his shoulders as he drove. "Maybe because there isn't much to talk about."

"Oh, yeah?" Sarah smirked. "I think we could find a few topics of conversation."

Aviva nudged her again, but Sarah squirmed away from her in the seat. She wasn't going to stop now.

"What would you like to talk about?" Jake asked.

Sarah sniffed. "Well, for one thing, I'd like to know what we did to offend you."

The boys glanced at each other again.

"*Well?*" she barked.

Jake glanced at her over his shoulder. His lips were pursed. "If you wanna know the truth, it pisses me off the way you say 'so-called' Promised Land." His fingers formed little quotation marks in the air. "You make it sound like we're looking for the Wizard of Oz or something. We're *not.*"

Sarah's face shriveled in disbelief. They were offended because she didn't believe in some phony Chosen One? She almost felt like laughing. "Are you serious?"

"Yeah." He nodded without a trace of humor. "I am."

Paul sighed. "Come on, Jake—"

"What?" he interrupted. He settled back in his seat. "*She* brought it up."

Sarah took a deep breath. She glanced at Aviva. The girl was pale, shaking her head again and again. *Oh, jeez.* What was Aviva so worried about? So they were arguing a little bit. Not even arguing—they were talking. Dialogue was good. Dialogue led to understanding. It was a lot better than sitting around and letting their emotions stew for another ten days.

"Listen, I didn't mean anything by it," Sarah muttered after a moment. "I'm sorry it bothered you. I won't let it happen again. Really."

"Whatever," Jake grumbled.

"Let me ask you something, though," Sarah said. "How do you know for sure that this Promised Land is real? I mean, have you heard rumors or something?"

Both boys snorted at the same time.

Sarah leaned forward. "Have you?"

"No," Jake mumbled. "But you wouldn't believe us if we told you the truth."

She raised her eyebrows. "Oh, yeah? Try me."

Jake's mouth pressed into a tight line.

"We had visions, all right?" Paul blurted. "We—"

"Visions?" Sarah gasped. She couldn't believe it. Why hadn't they said anything about it before? She cast an excited glance at Aviva. But for some reason, the girl looked more frightened and agitated than ever—swallowing, fidgeting in her seat. What was her problem? Now these guys would *have* to see the truth about this phony Chosen One. More important, they'd see the truth about *her.* Every Visionary Sarah had ever met ended up believing in her. And those who didn't, well . . . the scroll foretold that they would perish. She'd already seen a nonbeliever die once.

80

"Why didn't you tell us?" she asked.

"Because a lot of people think we're nuts," Jake mumbled.

"Why? Why are visions any more nuts than believing in a Promised Land and a Chosen One? A lot of people believe in that. Not just Visionaries. I mean, the rumor about the Promised Land spread as far as Ohio. What's crazier?"

Jake shifted in his seat. His eyes narrowed, flashing between her and Aviva. "Who *are* you guys, anyway?"

Sarah couldn't help but smile. "You wouldn't believe me if I told you the truth."

Jake looked at Paul. The minivan slowed slightly. Paul glanced in the rearview mirror. His back stiffened.

"Sarah, don't," Aviva whispered. "Please, don't—"

"It's okay," Sarah interrupted gently. "It'll clear the air between us once and for all—"

"Answer the question," Jake spat.

Sarah looked him straight in the eye. "I'm the Chosen One," she proclaimed.

"No, no!" Aviva cried. She buried her face in her hands. "Stop it! Please . . ."

Jake's expression remained the same, as if he were incapable of processing the information. "The Chosen One," he repeated dully.

"That's right." Sarah nodded, then frowned at Aviva. "*She* knows it."

"Sarah, *please.*" Aviva moaned.

Jake sneered. "It looks to me like she isn't so sure," he said.

"Well, I can prove it." Sarah shook her head. What

was wrong with Aviva, anyway? Back in Pennsylvania, *she* was the one who kept encouraging Sarah to tell the truth to as many people as possible, to spread the word and gain followers. Why the sudden change of heart—*now* of all times? It was utterly baffling, not to mention stupid and dangerous. But Sarah would prove she was the Chosen One . . . even if it meant harming one or both of these boys. She honestly didn't care anymore. She was sick of being denied everywhere she went. How could she be expected to defeat the Demon if no one believed in her?

"We're waiting," Jake muttered.

"Fine." She returned his stare. "If you have visions, then I know they involve one of two things. One of them is *me*. Obviously you aren't having those kinds of visions. So you must be having visions involving the Demon—"

The tires screeched. Sarah's head slammed against the back of Paul's seat.

The van jerked to an abrupt stop.

Paul whirled around. He was breathing heavily.

"What about the Demon?" he demanded.

Sarah rubbed her bruised forehead. She wasn't sure what to say. Paul suddenly looked as if he had gone insane; she could see the whites of his eyes.

"I-it . . . it could be a lot of things," she stammered. *Think!* She racked her memory for specific passages from the scroll. "It could be about how the Demon is going to lead the False Prophet astray, then betray him. Or it could be about how the Demon is going to use a traitor against the Chosen One—"

"My *God.*" Paul gasped. His face turned a sickly

white. He turned to Jake. "That's what I told you! Remember? I saw the traitor with no face. The one who betrays the Chosen One at the final battle—"

"One second, all right?" Jake cut in. His eyes flickered over Sarah's face for a moment. "What about the False Prophet?"

She shrugged. "I think it's obvious. This *so-called* Chosen One in this *so-called* Promised Land is the False Prophet." She jerked a finger at Aviva. "She's a Visionary, too. She had a vision right before you picked us up. She saw the Demon leading the False Prophet out of his phony kingdom. . . ."

Her voice trailed off. Jake was scowling, shaking his head.

"What?" She groaned.

"That's impossible."

"What's impossible?"

He shot a suspicious look at Aviva, whose trembling hands still covered her face. "She couldn't have had a vision," he whispered. "None of us have had any visions since the snow started. Not *one* Visionary we talked to."

Sarah glowered at him. "Well, *she* did."

Jake glanced back at Paul.

"Servants of the Demon," they whispered simultaneously.

Paul nodded. "There's no other way they would know."

"What are you *talking* about?" Sarah demanded.

But the boys didn't answer. Instead they flung both of their doors open and jumped out into the snow.

"Hey!" she protested. "What are you—"

Her own door crashed open. Sudden panic immobilized her. What were they *doing?* Paul grabbed her arm and savagely yanked her out of her seat. She tumbled into the slush on the side of the road, and cold wetness soaked through her clothes in an instant. She shivered and tried to brush herself clean. Doors slammed. Sarah froze. They couldn't be leaving her here. They couldn't.

"Wait!" she cried, whirling around. "Don't—"

The engine roared. Tires squealed—and the van bounced forward, spewing snow and mud into her face. She flinched.

"Stop!" she shrieked, sputtering. She caught a glimpse of Aviva lying on the opposite side of the highway. "Come back here! Come back. . . ."

The taillights disappeared into the snow.

"Come *back!*" she yelled again. But the cry was too hoarse, too soft.

Her shoulders sagged.

The boys were gone.

NINE

**Amarillo,
Texas
Afternoon of July 17**

The hourglass is almost empty.

I can see the last of the black sand trickling through the narrow funnel. There's so little time left. . . .

The Chosen One watches, too. She's right beside me. I can't see her face. She just watches. She doesn't make a move to stop the sand. She seems almost resigned to die.

"Do something!" I cry.

She shakes her head. "I can't, Julia. Not until you and I come together."

"Then show me your face," I plead. "Please. Show me your face."

"How can I show you my face when I don't even know it myself?"

Julia opened her eyes.

For a moment she wasn't sure if she were still trapped in the throes of the vision. It was so dark. She blinked a few times.

Gradually the grim surroundings took shape—the rough-hewn stone walls, the damp floor with its stinking hole, the few flickering candles . . . *the cellar.* Her heart squeezed painfully. Why hadn't she come to expect it? She always woke up in the same place. The pattern never changed. She would drift back to reality, disoriented for the briefest instant—and she would see them: Linda and the Healer, sitting directly across from her on those hard wooden folding chairs, staring at her, *studying* her.

Who are you? she would wonder.

And after a period of time—hours, minutes, *seconds*—she would slip into another vision, and the process would repeat itself, an endless circle of torture.

"What did you see?" the Healer asked.

Julia lowered her gaze. She couldn't stand to look at him.

"Share with us, Jules," Linda murmured. "It's for your own good."

Jules? Julia swallowed. Linda had no right calling her *Jules.* It was a term of endearment. Only her parents had called her that. And Luke, of course. But that didn't count.

Why did Linda and the Healer even bother to maintain this charade—that they were trying to help her? But she couldn't let her anger show. As long as she played her role, they would play theirs. It was a symbiotic relationship. She couldn't slip. Not once. No matter how badly the fear or outrage festered inside her, she *had* to pretend that she still believed the Healer was the Chosen One, that Linda was her friend. Otherwise she might end up like George.

"Julia, listen to me very carefully," the Healer

86

whispered. "When this first happened, you said that I was going to die. Why did you say that?"

"I—I don't know," she stammered. "I was just . . . scared."

"Scared of what?" he asked.

Scared of you, she thought—but she shrugged. She could feel those piercing blue eyes bearing down upon her. . . . She felt like a dying flower, wilting under the harsh rays of an unforgiving sun. Where did his power come from? He could perform miracles; he could even do the unimaginable, curing the plague with a touch. She'd seen it with her own eyes. She'd seen him pluck Luke from the brink of death, even as the flesh melted off Luke's face. *How?*

But she knew. Of course she knew. No matter how many times she asked herself that question, she always arrived at the same answer. It was as obvious as it was horrifying.

The Demon gives you your power.

For a few days, after the first vision of the true Chosen One struck her, she even considered the possibility that Harold Wurf *was* the Demon. But no—she knew that the Demon was female. Just like George said she was . . . A terrible, wrenching nausea seized her gut. *George.* He'd known the truth about Harold and the real Chosen One all along. He kept trying to tell her. He kept insisting that the Chosen One and the Demon were girls, but Julia refused to listen. And in the end, she'd trusted Harold's word over the word of the boy she loved.

If she hadn't, would George still be alive?

Probably. If she'd known then what she knew

now, the two of them would have escaped from this place. They would have gone west. They would have had hope for their baby—

Our baby!

No, no, no. She couldn't think about that. There was no point in asking what-if. She'd learned that long ago, even before the plague—back when she'd lost her parents, back when she'd been forced into a life of neglect and loneliness by a freak car accident. Asking what-if only drove a person crazy.

"Julia?" Linda asked in the lengthening silence. "Julia, are you okay?"

She took a deep breath. "I'm fine."

"What are you scared of?" Harold pressed.

Julia's eyes flashed to Linda. She gazed back with that same worried look she wore when Julia confessed that she was pregnant. But Linda didn't care about Julia or her baby. Everything she did or said was a lie.

Hold on.

A sickening thought dawned on her.

What if *Linda* was the Demon?

Was it possible? Linda *did* have an uncanny knack for showing up in certain places at certain opportune times: whenever Harold performed one of his miracles, whenever someone had a vision, whenever a nonbeliever challenged Harold's authority. And Linda was the one who'd reported George when he stole those pills. . . . *Good Lord.* George kept screaming about how he'd been framed, about how the whole theft was a setup. Julia's stomach lurched again. Linda had probably orchestrated the whole thing—

"What are you *scared* of?" Harold repeated. His voice hardened. "Answer me."

She swallowed, keeping her gaze fixed on Linda. "I . . . I . . ."

"Julia, I don't mean to be rude, but I'm running out of patience," he stated. "We've been asking you the same questions for *weeks*. If there's something you want to tell me, now is the time to do it."

"I . . . I want to go west," Julia finally managed. "I told you that."

Before she even knew what she was doing, she pushed herself out of her chair and began to pace back and forth across the uneven concrete. She couldn't help herself. If she sat still anymore, she'd lose her mind. Her eyes flashed to the door. She'd been tempted many times to try to break out of here. It wouldn't be hard; the weeks of snow had practically destroyed the wood. But trying now would be suicide, of course. She brushed a few strands of hair out of her eyes and began chewing on a thumbnail. What had George done when he'd been trapped down here? Had he gone insane, too?

At least he vaporized. At least his suffering ended quickly.

"The *Demon* wants you to go west," Linda whispered. "You have to accept that, Jules. You have to come to terms with the fact that the Demon is manipulating you. Just think about it. Visionaries keep coming to the Promised Land, but none of them is having visions. Two more showed up today. They said that they were almost stopped by the Demon's helpers on the way here. Can't you see that the

Demon wants us to go before the sign comes? Can't you—"

"Well, when is it going to *come?*" Julia wailed. "When? I'm sick of waiting, okay?"

Linda sighed. "I wish I knew," she murmured. "I wish—"

The door burst open.

It slammed against the opposite wall, rattling with a *smack*. Julia flinched.

Luke stood in the doorway—shivering, lips parted, hands raised in the air. His blistered face was the color of ice . . . except that he was drenched in some kind of thick crimson liquid. It dripped from his white robe, pooling on the floor at his feet.

"Blood," he croaked. "It's all blood."

Oh, no. Julia felt her gorge rise. *He killed someone.*

"What's going on?" Harold demanded. "What have you *done?*"

"Not me. The sky. The sky . . ." All at once Luke burst into tears. He sank to his knees and slumped against the door frame, trembling with convulsive sobs. "The sky . . ."

Julia froze. *The sky?*

"It's the sign!" Linda suddenly shrieked. "Come on!" In a flash she was out of her chair and brushing past Julia—nearly knocking her to the floor. She hurtled over Luke and scrambled up the steps. "Come on! This is it!"

For a few seconds Julia just stood there as Harold clambered after Linda and disappeared upstairs. Her breath came in uneven gasps. She couldn't tear her gaze from Luke. After all these years, he'd finally succumbed to madness. It was terrifying—but at the same time oddly fascinating. In spite of her shock and horror, she felt vindicated. He really *was* a psychopath. And now all the world could see the truth.

"Luke?" she whispered. "What did you do?"

"Nothing!" he cried. "I told you—it's the sky."

Julia bit her lip. From somewhere upstairs drifted the faraway sound of shouting voices. She couldn't quite hear what they were saying—but the message was very clear.

They were terrified.

Her heart began to pound.

"Go see for yourself," Luke murmured.

Julia kept staring at him. And after a long moment her feet began to shuffle toward the staircase, as if they were moving of their own free will. She'd been waiting to get out of this pit for weeks now, *praying* for it. But now that the opportunity was upon her, she didn't feel nearly as relieved as she'd thought she would.

She cringed slightly as she slunk past Luke, edging as far away from him as possible, then ducked through the narrow doorway. *Clomp . . . clomp . . . clomp . . .* Up the stairs she trudged, following the path of Luke's bloody footprints to the first floor—

My God!

There was a huge red stain on Harold's front hall rug. It spilled out onto the door frame. Bile rose in her throat. And she could hear something else now, too, something over the moan of those tortured voices. It was the unmistakable patter of heavy rain.

"The sign has come!" Linda cried just outside the

open door. She sounded ecstatic, as if she were in a trance. "The sign! This is it, Jules! We can go west now! We can face the Demon! It's time!"

Julia lifted her head.

She stopped breathing.

It wasn't snowing anymore.

No. Something new was falling from the sky. And it fell in a wild torrent—washing away the blanket of whiteness, swirling in the fields, forming puddles in the dirt road . . . purging every tree and bush of their icicles. The temperature climbed. *Fast.* Droplets of sweat moistened Julia's forehead. A lightning bolt split the gray sky. Seconds later a crack of thunder shook the house—the kind of deafening crack one might hear during any average thunderstorm in the middle of July.

Only it wasn't an average thunderstorm.

It was a shower of blood.

Thick, warm blood. Julia could smell the coppery odor. And she had just one thought as she gaped at Linda and Harold, watching their upturned faces transform into something inhuman with a mask of rich red.

Luke is sane after all.

PART III;

July 18-31

**Old Pine Mall,
Babylon, Washington
Morning of July 18**

"I'm telling you, Caleb, it's *over,*" Jezebel murmured with a smile. "Come on. You can't stay in here forever."

Caleb frowned. What was the problem with staying in here forever? He loved toy stores. Especially this one. He was really starting to dig this place. He could sit on this dusty carpet for another ten years. Besides, he was having a blast—staring at his twisted reflection in those wacky mirrors, trying on different masks, playing with the action figures (the coolest thing was making Aquaman and Shaquille O'Neal battle each other kung fu style), drinking peppermint schnapps. . . .

"Well, *I'm* going outside," Jezebel stated.

She stood up and stretched. Her long-sleeved black T-shirt came untucked. Caleb caught a glimpse of her taut, white stomach. He quickly lowered his eyes.

What have I done?

He was *not* going to fool around with her anymore. Period. End of story. As a matter of fact, he was going to take a vow of celibacy right now. *I hereby give up sex forever. I am The Monk of Toyland. That's right.* The old Caleb Walker was dead. He swallowed nervously. This past month had been a freak accident, a mistake. It wasn't his fault. He'd been *trapped* with this chick. First the blizzard, and then . . . and then . . .

"What's wrong?" Jezebel asked. She yawned. "You look kinda greenish."

"How the hell am I *supposed* to look?" He glowered at her. "Call me crazy, but when it starts raining blood, my skin loses that healthy Oil of Olay glow."

Jezebel rolled her eyes. "But it *stopped*. That's what I'm trying to tell you."

"How do you *know*, Jezebel?" he cried. He waved his hands around the shadowy, candlelit room. "In case you hadn't noticed, there aren't any windows in here. Or do you have X-ray vision?"

She giggled. "Come on. I've got a sixth sense for this kind of thing. I thought you would've learned that by now."

He looked down at the floor.

"Don't tell me you're *scared.*" She moaned.

Oh, shut up. He shook his head. If she got her kicks by insulting him, fine. He didn't give a crap. Because when he looked back on all the sordid events of his life, he could still pride himself on one crucial strong point: He was not a wimp. A drunk, maybe. A drug addict . . . well, possibly. A bum, *definitely.* But one thing was certain. He never let fear dictate his actions. He never backed away from a sketchy situation. Even on New Year's Eve—when everybody around him was either throwing a fit or melting into goo—even *then* he kept his cool.

Only . . . this was different. This was heavy. This was major, end-of-the-world, apocalyptic, wrath-of-God stuff. He didn't *understand* this. Not that he understood the plague, of course. But at least there might be some sort of scientific explanation for what had happened.

Nothing could explain raining blood.

In fact, the only way it made any sense—to *him*, at least—was that this was all some kind of divine punishment for the way he'd been cheating on Ariel for the past month.

Yeah, right. It was all directed at Caleb Walker. The sad truth was, he wasn't important enough to have anything to do with this stuff. And he knew it. No, if the universe was finally falling apart, he'd just end up becoming a statistic—another tally mark on the side of the losers.

"You really *are* scared, aren't you?" Jezebel asked.

"Aren't you?" he grumbled.

"Nope," she said. "Like I told you, it's over. There's no point in obsessing over it or anything. Listen, why don't we just go take a look, all right? We'll go to that huge skylight in the food court. It won't kill you to *look.*"

Caleb grunted. But he didn't budge.

"Oh, man." She sighed impatiently. "Caleb, do you know what agoraphobia is?"

Great, he thought. *More weird psychobabble.* He glanced up at her. "No," he answered in a dull voice. "Please tell me, Jezebel. I'm dying to know."

"It's a fear of getting out in the open," she stated. "It's this mental disease where you stay

97

cooped up in one place all the time because you're so scared that—"

"I *get* it," he snapped. He hopped to his feet and marched past her—between two narrow rows of shelves and straight for the door. Why couldn't she just keep her mouth shut? Or better yet, why didn't she leave him alone? Why did she always have to push him into something he didn't want to do? He didn't ask for this. All he wanted was for things to get back to normal, *before* he met Jezebel, *before* kids started melting whenever they got near his girlfriend.

"Hey!" Jezebel called. "Where are you going?"

"Where do you think?" he yelled over his shoulder. "I'm going to see if you're right."

"That's more like it!" She bounded down the aisle and threw her arms around his neck. "There's the Caleb I know and love—"

"Don't *touch* me!" he barked. He shoved her away from him, nearly knocking her to the floor. "I mean it."

She frowned. Then her lips curled in a smirk. "Uh . . . Caleb? It's a little too late to worry about catching cooties, don't you think?"

He glared back at her, clenching his fists at his sides. He'd never hit a girl before, never even *considered* it, but right now. . . . He exhaled and glanced out into the dark hall. His stomach turned slightly. Most of the tile floor was splattered with brownish red muck. A rank, salty stench wafted through the doorway. So much blood . . .

"Hey, I didn't mean to make you feel *stupid* or anything," Jezebel teased. "I learned about agoraphobia in

98

this intro to psych course that I took with your ex-girlfriend. It was—"

"She's *not* my ex-girlfriend," Caleb interrupted. He whirled to face her. "Got it?"

Jezebel cocked her eyebrow. "I see," she murmured sarcastically. "I guess we're feeling a little touchy today. How would *you* describe Ariel?"

"I'd take the 'ex' out," he snarled.

She clucked her tongue disapprovingly. "Well . . . that's a problem, Caleb. I mean, I know Ariel pretty well. She's open-minded, but I don't know if she'd go for sharing her boyfriend. Especially with me. We kinda have this history, you know? Would *you* be psyched if you learned that Ariel was screwing someone *you* hated for the past month?"

You bitch! White-hot rage flashed through Caleb. She was going to tell Ariel, wasn't she? Every muscle in his body tensed—as if he had suddenly been pumped full of electricity. But he summoned what was left of his self-control and jerked a finger in her face. "Don't you dare say anything to Ariel," he growled. "Don't you even *think* it." Without another word, he stormed out into the blood-slicked hall, straight toward the food court.

"I don't know what you're so upset about," Jezebel said, scurrying to catch up with him. "What has Ariel ever done for *you?* She took you away from home. And so far, all she's done is blow you off for her new best buddy. It's not exactly—"

"Go to hell," he snapped, picking up his pace.

"But you haven't even seen her in, like, two weeks!" she cried, laughing. "No offense, but it's not the healthiest relationship in the world. Why do you care about it so much? I told you, Caleb—that chick is bad news. You have no idea *how* bad."

He stopped and spun around. "Just *shut up*, okay? I'm sick of . . ." His voice trailed off.

A couple of kids were running toward them down the hall. Their clothes were rust colored from blood. His eyes narrowed. They were smiling, but their faces seemed twisted somehow, as if they were tripping on acid or something.

"The Chosen One cleared the skies!" one of them shrieked as they raced past him and Jezebel. "It's all over! The rain is over!"

Caleb stared at them as they skidded around a corner and disappeared in the direction of the food court.

"See?" Jezebel murmured, sounding very pleased with herself. "I *told* you."

A nervous twitter flashed through Caleb's stomach. He glanced back at Jezebel, then hurried after the two kids. *There's no way she could be right. There's no way she could have known that without going outside.*

But as soon as he rounded the corner, he saw that the cracks between the double doors that opened onto the food court were suffused with a dazzling light.

He broke into a jog. He hadn't seen light that bright in *weeks*. Light like that could only come from one source, one source only. . . .

He burst through the doors.

He couldn't see a thing. He blinked and squinted,

raising a hand to shield his eyes from the brightness. Shouting voices filled the air. There was a steady dripping noise like the sound of a dozen leaky faucets. Every surface gleamed: the bloodstained marble floor, the plastic tables, the dry fountain. . . . Caleb's eyes watered. A few kids jostled him, but he hardly noticed. Holding his breath, he cautiously lifted his gaze to the huge domed skylight, towering overhead. . . .

"The sun!" he yelled.

He caught a fleeting glimpse of it—that blinding white orb against a cloudless blue sky—and his eyes squeezed shut. Shapeless red patterns danced under the lids. His hand fell to his side. The intense heat and glow began to warm his face. He started laughing. He couldn't help himself. It was over. The snow, the blood . . . all of it. Summer was here again!

"I don't want to gloat or anything, but what did I tell you?"

Jezebel. Her voice was suddenly right beside him. He turned and peered at her out of the corner of his stinging eyes. The wild surge of joy began to subside—replaced with a strange and sudden fear. She had *known.* Somehow she had known that it was over. . . .

"See?" she said with a proud smile. "No more blood."

He let out a deep, shaky breath. "How did you . . ." He didn't finish.

She laughed. "Haven't you figured out who you're dealing with yet?"

"The sign!" some guy yelled behind him, cutting

her off. "It's the sign! The nonbelievers will die! The Chosen One will prevail! It's the sign of her promise!"

Jezebel snorted. "Oh, give me a break. This isn't a sign about the *Chosen One.*"

Caleb stared at her, baffled. "What do you mean?"

She shrugged nonchalantly. "It's what I've been trying to tell you all along. If all this stuff is a sign about anything, it's that something bad is in Babylon. Why do you think all these weirdos came here in the first place? Why do you think the rain and snow ended? It's because people are beginning to see the truth about who *she* is."

"Sh-she?" Caleb stammered. His blood ran cold. This conversation wasn't making any sense. "What are you talking about?"

Jezebel looked him straight in the face. "Oh, come on, Caleb. You're not as dumb as you look."

"Maybe I am," he said in a hollow voice.

"Who else?" she cried. *"Ariel."*

ELEVEN

**Amarillo,
Texas
Morning of July 23**

Entering the Promised Land! Submit to the Healer and He Will Grant You Eternal Life!

Sarah squinted up at the spray-painted billboard.

She supposed she should have felt *something*—some kind of shock or outrage or indignation. Or maybe just relief that they'd finally made it to this place . . . after being dumped in the snow and drenched in blood for an entire day, among other things. But she was too tired. She swayed slightly and wiped the sweat from her brow. Then she glanced back at Aviva.

"What do you think?" she croaked. Her throat was so parched, she could hardly swallow. "This is the third sign we've seen in an hour. This must be the place."

Aviva stood on her tiptoes, peering past the

billboard across a huge, barren stretch of dry dirt. "I guess so," she murmured uncertainly. "I mean, I can see something up there. . . ."

Sarah followed Aviva's gaze. Up ahead, maybe a quarter mile from the sun-broiled highway, stood a squat red tower, a dilapidated brown barn, and a little wood frame house. *Wow.* She hadn't even noticed that before. Or maybe she had. Maybe she'd just been expecting something a little more impressive. *This* was it? The fabled Promised Land? The magic place whose legend had spread across the entire country? For some reason, she'd imagined a grand oasis—like Ibrahim's palace in the Egyptian desert. Not some dumpy little farm. They'd endured weeks of hell just to come here?

"It looks deserted," Aviva muttered. She absently tugged on one of the straps of her backpack. "The False Prophet must have already left. I *knew* it." She scowled. "As soon as it stopped raining blood, I knew he would leave. That was the sign. You shouldn't have said anything to those guys in the car. We would have gotten here when there was still time—"

"How do *you* know?" Sarah interrupted flatly. "If that was a sign, you should have told me. And for all we know, those guys never made it. For all we know, this place *isn't* deserted. Don't you think we should actually take a look around before we give up?"

Aviva sighed. "Fine." She groaned. She struck out into the dead field, making a beeline for the buildings.

What is her problem? Sarah wondered angrily. Aviva *never* used to second-guess her. But somewhere between Pennsylvania and Texas, Aviva had suffered a major personality disorder. Gone was the whiny, timid little mouse—the girl whose unquestioning adoration of Sarah practically drove Sarah crazy. Now it seemed as if Aviva didn't have any respect for Sarah at all. If she still believed that Sarah was the Chosen One, she sure didn't *show* it. Maybe she was a schizophrenic or something.

"So are you coming or what?" Aviva called over her shoulder.

Sarah glared back at her, but she started walking. Little motes of dust danced past her in the dry air, flashing like tiny fireflies in the sun. Her glasses fogged. Even if this place *was* deserted, it would provide them with some shade and a place to rest. That was *something*. If she kept walking in this heat any longer, she would drop dead. One week she was freezing, the next she was burning up. It was kind of ironic, wasn't it? She actually found herself missing the snow. All that water had just melted and evaporated into nothingness. What a waste.

"Hey!" Aviva suddenly cried. "I see somebody!" She tried to run, waving her hands over her head, but the backpack weighed her down. She almost looked like a hunchback. "Hey, you!" she shouted. "Hey!"

I told you we should check it out. Sarah shook her head. She paused for a moment and wiped her lenses on her grubby T-shirt. So maybe they'd end up meeting this False Prophet after all. Maybe Aviva would realize that she really *had* been a jerk.

But when Sarah put her glasses back on, she saw that Aviva had stopped in her tracks. Her head was bowed.

"What's wrong?" Sarah called.

"It's not a person," Aviva snapped. "It's a *scarecrow.*"

A smile crossed Sarah's face. She bit her lip to keep from laughing. *Serves you right,* she thought. "Hey, don't feel so bad." She walked up to Aviva and patted her on the shoulder. "It fools birds, too—"

"It's not funny," Aviva snarled.

Sarah folded her arms across her chest and raised her eyebrows. "All right. Do you want to tell me what's bothering you? Because you're really starting to get on my nerves."

Aviva took a deep breath. Her jaw tightened. She blinked once, then averted her eyes. "I told you," she grumbled. She resumed her plodding march toward the farm. "You shouldn't have told those guys you were the Chosen One—"

"Excuse me," Sarah interrupted. "But I *am* the Chosen One. Remember?"

But Aviva just kept walking. "Right," she said dully. "You're the Chosen One."

"Hey—look at me!" Sarah barked, running up alongside her. "In case you forgot, *you* were the one who told me that I needed to spread the word and get followers. Any reason you changed your mind?"

Aviva sniffed. She kept her eyes pinned to the dirt. "I meant you should get followers *after* we got here. *After* people saw who you were and what you could do. I mean . . . didn't you learn anything when we were on the boat?"

"The boat?" Sarah cried. "What's that supposed to mean? *Everybody* on that boat believed in me!"

"Not at first," Aviva pointed out. "When you first

got on board, they threw you down in the holding pen. They only started believing in you *after* the scroll was lit on fire and didn't get burned. After they saw real magic."

Sarah shook her head. Her footsteps grew more violent, kicking up dust. *"Wrong,* Aviva. They only believed in me after that boy told me I *wasn't* the Chosen One and melted. It even was in the scroll: 'Those who deny the Chosen One will perish.' And—"

"What about those guys in the van, then?" Aviva cut in. Her voice began to tremble. "They didn't believe you were the Chosen One. And they were fine. They were fine enough to ditch us in the middle of a blizzard."

Sarah stopped short. "So what are you saying?" she whispered. "Are you saying you don't believe in me?"

Aviva sighed. "I believe in you, Sarah," she murmured. "It's just that . . . we don't have the scroll, you know? So we have to be careful. I mean, maybe that prophecy about people who deny the Chosen One was just for that lunar cycle. Who knows? Maybe *nothing* will happen to people who deny you now. Without the prophecies right here in front of us, it's impossible to know. It's impossible to know *anything.*"

Sarah stared back at her. Her mind raced, but she couldn't think of one single argument, one possible way to refute what Aviva was saying. An unpleasant numbness filled her gut. Aviva was right. They were blind without the scroll. Their only hope now was to pray that Aviva had another vision of the prophecies in the near future. . . .

"Look, I don't mean to be harsh or anything," Aviva stated quietly. "I'm just telling you what I think. And right now, I think we should check this place out and get going as quickly as possible. It's pretty obvious that there's nobody here. But maybe they left a clue as to where they were headed."

"Um . . . okay," Sarah muttered, nodding. There wasn't much more to say.

Aviva started back toward the property.

Sarah followed a few paces behind her. The seconds ticked by in silence. The queasiness in Sarah's stomach seemed to expand, spreading throughout her limbs. So much uncertainty lay ahead. . . .

She glanced up. *What kind of a dump is this?* As the buildings drew closer, she could see that they were in worse shape than she'd thought. Shingles were falling off the house. Windows were broken. The roof of the barn sloped inward; it was on the verge of collapse. And something had been painted on the side of the silo—but the letters had been washed away, dripping down the wall in a stream of illegible gibberish.

"Want to check the house first?" Aviva asked.

Sarah shrugged. "Sure."

Aviva slung her pack down into the dirt, and the two of them marched up the rickety porch steps. The floorboards creaked. The wood seemed to give under Sarah's feet as she approached the front door, which dangled precariously from three ancient, rusted hinges.

"I guess I should knock," Aviva mumbled. She rapped on the frame once, very softly.

There was no answer.

She glanced back at Sarah. "Well?"

"Let's just go in," Sarah muttered. She leaned forward and gently pushed open the door. The hinges squealed loudly, as if they were crying out in pain. Sarah winced. On second thought, maybe they should leave. The whole house looked as if it might fall into dust at any second. It was starting to give Sarah the creeps. But Aviva stepped inside.

Sarah followed her into a dark, musty front hall. The rug on the floor was filthy—covered in some sort of blackish muck. Dried blood, maybe. A cracked mirror hung on one wall, facing a narrow door on the other.

All at once, Aviva froze. She turned back to Sarah and lifted a finger to her lips. "Do you hear that?" she mouthed.

Sarah paused. She *did* hear something . . . a rattling sound. She strained her ears.

Aviva tiptoed down the hall a few more feet, then glanced back at Sarah. "Somebody's here," she mouthed. She leaned close to the wall and slunk around the corner.

Sarah's pulse picked up a few beats. *Great. Maybe those two jerks who tossed us out on the highway warned the False Prophet that we were coming. . . .* But there was no point in inventing horrible scenarios. She forced herself to inch forward and peer around the corner.

A lone door loomed at the end of a narrow corridor, open a crack. Aviva glanced back at Sarah and pointed to the opening. The noise grew louder, more intense. It was clearly coming from behind that door. Only now it seemed to be more of a *scraping* sound. . . .

"Come on," Aviva whispered, beckoning.

Sarah crept up beside her.

"What should we do?" Aviva hissed.

Well, we're here, Sarah thought. *We might as well take a look.* Gathering her courage, she strode forward and flung open the door.

A foul stench instantly assailed her nostrils.

She cringed. So this was the kitchen. And judging from the food-stained floor, the grimy cabinets, and the dishes piled high in the sink, *something* had been left to rot—

"Look!" Aviva whispered.

Sarah jumped. *My God . . .*

A disheveled boy in a filthy white robe was sitting at the kitchen table, furiously spooning plain grape jelly from a glass jar into his mouth. So *that's* where the noise was coming from. He looked to be about fifteen or sixteen . . . her brother's age—only his features were cold and hard. Long, greasy blond hair hung in his face. He couldn't have been more than ten feet away. But if he noticed them, he didn't bother to acknowledge it.

Finally, after several seconds, he looked up.

"Yeah?" he grunted.

Sarah blinked. He had striking green eyes . . . and she couldn't help but notice how sharply they contrasted with the dull pallor of his sallow, sunken cheeks. She tried to smile. "We're, um . . . we're looking for—"

"Harold?" he interrupted. "He's not here."

Harold? Sarah glanced at Aviva, then back at the boy. "Who's that?"

The boy sneered. "You're trying to tell me you don't know?"

"Who are you?" Aviva asked.

"Somebody who doesn't believe in Harold's bull." He started gobbling up the jelly again. His gaze flashed between the two of them.

Sarah shook her head. "Look, I'm really sorry, but . . . uh, we don't know . . ."

The boy set the jar down on the table with a sharp thud. His eyes narrowed, zeroing in on Sarah with an animal intensity. "Harold didn't send you back to make sure I was really dead?"

"I—I don't know any Harold," Sarah stammered.

He frowned. "Then what are you doing here?"

"Well, we thought that, uh, maybe we could find . . ."

"The Chosen One," Aviva finished.

The boy sighed. "You're not gonna find her *here,* that's for sure."

Sarah hesitated. "Do you know about the Chosen One?" she asked cautiously.

"I know she isn't Harold Wurf," he mumbled, slouching back in his chair.

"But you know that she's a girl," Sarah pressed. Sudden excitement surged through her veins. "You said 'she.' How do you know that?"

"Why don't you tell me who *you* are first," he spat back at her. "How's that?"

Uh-oh. Sarah's eyes flashed to Aviva again.

Aviva stepped forward. "I'm a Visionary," she stated. "And I have a feeling you are, too."

He gazed back at her. He didn't utter a word. Sarah held her breath, glancing between the two of them. Neither of them blinked. Her throat tightened. Was it so smart to tell him the truth? What if he reacted violently—like those two boys?

"Maybe I am," he finally whispered.

Sarah breathed a small sigh of relief. At least he didn't lunge at them or make a sudden move for a knife. That was something.

"What happened here?" Aviva asked.

He shook his head and scowled. "Harold managed to convince everyone that *he* was the Chosen One. Even Visionaries. Everybody except me."

"I don't understand," Aviva said, casting a quick glance at Sarah. "Where did he go?"

"Out west, I guess." The boy shrugged. "I'm not really sure. I've been hiding out in the woods. I didn't come back until today. He probably split when the snow turned to blood." He smirked. "Knowing Harold, he twisted the blood thing to make it seem like *he* made it happen. Either that or the Demon did it, and she gave Harold the credit. . . ."

The Prophecies! Sarah gasped. That was written in the scroll! There was a line from the fifth lunar cycle; she remembered it very clearly. . . . *"The servants of the Demon will produce miracle after miracle, attributing signs and wonders to the False Prophet."* Raining blood certainly qualified as a miracle. The boy hadn't quoted the stanza word for word, but he'd summed it up pretty concisely. Yup. He *had* to be a

Visionary. There was no other way he could have known something like that.

"What?" he asked, furrowing his brow.

"Nothing," Sarah muttered apologetically. "Sorry. So did this 'Harold' guy know you were on to him? Did you tell him that you didn't believe in him?"

The boy nodded. "That's why I had to hide. I had to make it seem like I melted."

Sarah's eyes widened. *"Melted?* How did you do that?"

"It wasn't easy. I had to crawl through a stinking hole in the floor I used as a toilet. Right through my own . . . anyway, I had to do it late at night, when nobody was up. I found a big vat of some old, rotten pig feed. It stunk. It looked like black tar. I rolled around in it." He laughed, very harshly—and his face darkened. "Later, I snuck into the kitchen and found a bunch of cans of refried black beans. That was the finishing touch. I left my clothes in a pile on the floor in all that muck and crawled back through the toilet. . . ."

Sarah's stomach squeezed. She glanced at Aviva. Her face was pale.

"I'm sorry," Sarah murmured. "That was a very . . . a very brave thing to do."

He blinked. "Really?" He sounded embarrassed. "Uh . . . thanks."

Sarah allowed herself a smile. Maybe this boy wasn't as tough as he pretended to be.

"Anyway, I'm gonna go out west and track him down," he went on. "My girlfriend is still . . ." He shook his head. "She's still with him. I gotta get her back."

"Maybe we can help," Sarah said gently. "What's your name? Mine's Sarah."

He suddenly broke into a grin—and the whole character of his face changed, as if he were now bathed in a soft light. The transformation was remarkable. When he smiled, he looked almost *sweet* . . . younger, more innocent, more playful.

He trusts us now. He knows we aren't going to hurt him.

"My name's George Porter," he said. "And yeah, sure. You can help me. Why not? I can use all the help I can get."

TWELVE

**Babylon,
Washington
July 24–31**

Even after the snow melted, and the blood stopped falling from the sky, and Babylon suddenly found itself in the midst of a balmy, cloudless, tourist-season summer . . . even after an entire week of beautiful weather, Ariel refused to leave her house.

She barely even left her room. She spent most of the days sitting alone by the window, staring down at the sun-dappled pavement of Puget Drive and wondering if some Chosen One freak was going to break down the door and kill her. She was certain it would happen. Absolutely. It wasn't a matter of *if*. It was a matter of *when*.

And she didn't even care that much.

She figured it this way: She was going to die pretty soon anyway, right? She had three more years, tops. That was the *best*-case scenario.

It wasn't as if she had a hell of a lot to live for, either. Her boyfriend had essentially dumped her. Okay, he hadn't actually said the *words* or anything—but he hadn't even come near her house in over a week, so the message was pretty damn clear. Yup. Not a whole lot of uncertainty there. And the former queen of

Babylon High had been banished to loserdom. She had one friend left. Why did Leslie even bother hanging out with her? Not only was it a drag, but it was potentially life threatening. After all, Ariel still had the necklace. Those COFs still wanted it. For all she knew, they'd try to do something to Leslie just to get to *her*.

What's happening to me? she kept asking herself.

But not until she saw Jezebel happily strolling down the street one morning (in her hip black getup, as always) did Ariel figure out the answer. She didn't know *how* it had happened, of course—but she knew what she had become.

She had become Jezebel.

There was no denying it. Now *she* was the town freak. Even her skin was starting to look like Jezebel's: pasty, toneless, and dead white. Leslie had once described Jez as "a vampire with a day pass." Ariel was one, too. Not even. She was just a vampire, a ghost. Period.

"I'm worried about you," Leslie told her the next afternoon.

Ariel shrugged. "I'm fine."

"You're not *fine*, Ariel. You haven't gotten out of bed all day."

"So?" She groaned. She collapsed back down on her soft mattress and pulled the covers over her head. *Pee-ew.* Her nose wrinkled. She was really going to have to wash these sheets soon. But the process of cleaning things by hand was way too tedious. It also meant leaving the confines of her home to go to Edmunds Creek, something she was *not* prepared to do—

Leslie tore the blankets off her and flung them onto the rug.

"Hey!" Ariel protested, scowling.

"You have to get some fresh air," Leslie stated. She marched over to the window and shoved it open with a grunt. "It's way too stuffy in here. Just come outside for a couple of minutes."

Ariel leaned back against her pillows and sighed. A soft breeze tickled her nose, carrying the scent of pine with it. It *would* be nice to get out of here . . . even just to stretch. Her body felt totally limp and shapeless, like an industrial-size bag of dog food. She had bags under her eyes the size of golf balls.

"What if I run into a COF?" Ariel muttered.

Leslie blinked. She glanced out the window, fiddling distractedly with a strand of her long black hair. Once again, Ariel felt that heaviness in her head . . . that despair that hung over her like a shroud. Wouldn't it be nice to trade places with Leslie? Just for a day? To look like her and act like her? Wouldn't it be nice to have her flawless, tanned skin and those dazzling, dark eyes—that perfect body? To walk down the street without having to worry that somebody might vaporize . . .

"Let's just go out in your backyard," Leslie finally suggested. She was obviously trying her best to sound cheerful.

"You think it's gonna happen, too," Ariel whispered. Her voice quivered. "Don't you? You think a

COF is gonna come up to me and try to get my neck-lace and—"

"Hey, that reminds me," Leslie interrupted in a matter-of-fact tone. "I have something to show you."

Ariel shook her head violently. "Don't try to change the subject. This is—"

"I'm *not,*" Leslie soothed. She dug into the pocket of her tight skirt and pulled out a crumpled scrap of paper. "I found this on your front hall floor. Somebody must have slipped it under the door." She shrugged and handed it to Ariel. "Take a look."

Wonderful, Ariel thought, silently groaning. *It's probably a threatening letter.* She unfolded the note and frowned.

Dear Leslie,

I have important information about your friend Ariel. She is not what she seems. Meet me by the elevator doors on the seventh floor of Old Pine Mall this Saturday night, July 31, at 10 P.M. Come alone. This is *not a joke.*

—A Believer

"What do you think?" Leslie asked.

Ariel laughed grimly. "Nice of them to leave it in *my* house." She rolled her eyes and tossed it aside, watching it flutter to the floor with the rest of her garbage. "I guess people figured out that I'm not in the habit of leaving my room, huh?"

"Well, that's the thing." Leslie sat on the foot of the bed, then glanced down at the note, knitting her brow. "I figure it's gotta be somebody who knows you well. You know, somebody who's walked by your house and looked up at your window." She turned to Ariel. "I'm placing bets on that chick Jezebel."

Hmmm. Ariel thought for a minute, then shook her head. "Nah . . . Jezebel wouldn't be so businesslike. She wouldn't say: 'Saturday, July 31, at 10 P.M.' She'd just say: 'Saturday night.'" A smirk crossed Ariel's lips. "Besides, why would she want to meet with *you?* She likes you about as much as she likes pink leg warmers."

"Exactly," Leslie grumbled. Her eyes wandered toward the window. "She probably wants me to go there so she can stick a knife in my back."

Ariel leaned over and patted Leslie's shoulder. "Don't worry. She's not that smart. Or coordinated."

Leslie frowned at her—and the two of them burst into laughter.

"I'm sorry," Leslie mumbled after a few seconds. "I shouldn't have even showed you that stupid thing—"

"No, no, I'm glad you did," Ariel reassured her. "It . . . you know, it made me laugh." Her smile grew strained, then it faded altogether. "Not a whole lot makes me laugh these days, you know?"

Leslie nodded. "I know," she whispered.

"So what are you gonna do about it?"

"Do?" Leslie repeated. "What do you mean?"

"Are you gonna go meet this person?" Ariel asked, raising her eyebrows suggestively. "Maybe he's hot. Maybe he's got a body that just won't quit—"

"Ariel, *please.*" Leslie moaned. "Come on. . . ." She bit her lip. Then her eyes narrowed.

"Uh-oh," Ariel mumbled. "You have that weird look on your face."

Leslie stared at her. "You should come with me," she said slowly. "You should come hear what this anonymous jerk has to say about you."

Ariel swallowed. "You're, ah . . . you're joking, right?"

"Just listen, okay? It'll be—"

"Are you crazy?" Ariel cried. "I don't even want to go *downstairs*. What makes you think I want to schlep all the way to Old Pine Mall just to hear somebody talk trash about me? Besides, the person who wrote that note is obviously a COF. And if *I* go, then they'll . . . then they'll . . ." She couldn't bring herself to complete the sentence.

Then they'll catch the plague. They'll die right in front of me. Again.

A silence fell over the room.

"Maybe something *will* happen to them," Leslie muttered after a long moment. "But you know what?" She looked Ariel straight in the eye. "It'll serve them right for spreading lies about you. It'll serve them right for trying to turn somebody against their own best friend."

Saturday came a lot sooner than Ariel wanted it to.

The night was crisp and clear, full of stars. She supposed she should have felt invigorated—but she wasn't. The walk to the mall exhausted her. And even that was nothing compared to the climb up the darkened stairwell to the seventh floor. Leslie led the way, holding a candle. By the time Ariel reached the top, she could hardly stand. Man, was she out of shape. Of course, she'd hardly *moved* in weeks. Moping in bed didn't exactly qualify as an aerobic activity. She felt like a five-hundred-pound, sixty-year-old woman. Who smoked.

"Are you okay?" Leslie whispered. She didn't sound the slightest bit winded. It figured.

"Fine," Ariel gasped breathlessly. "You owe me big time, you know that?"

Leslie tried to smile, but it was clear even in the dim light of the candle that she was nervous. "I know," she murmured. She pushed open the door.

Ariel followed her out onto the balcony. A peculiar nostalgia swept over her. She hadn't been up to this part of the mall since she was a little girl . . . but of course, it looked much different in the daytime, back when the world was normal. Now it was dark and silent and void of people. She stood on her tiptoes and caught a glimpse of the bonfires in the food court, far below. She shook her head. All at once she felt very empty inside. People were still partying down there. And for some reason, she had a feeling she'd never be a part of it again.

"Which way are the elevators?" Leslie whispered.

Ariel glanced to her left and peered into the blackness. "I think that way—"

"Ariel?" a voice barked behind her. "What the hell are *you* doing here?"

Trevor!

She spun around and saw his tall, gangly frame in the shadows to the right. He was clutching a rifle. Her heart jumped. *The note!* Of course. Why hadn't she figured it out? Only a dork like Trevor would *type* a note. . . . But she knew why she hadn't thought of him. She never thought of Trevor unless she had to. People never thought of the ones they hated—unless the hated ones were right before their eyes.

Like now.

He took a step forward. "Get out of here," he snarled. "This is between me and Leslie."

"Get off it." Ariel groaned. "Whatever you're trying to pull, it's not—"

"I'm serious." He cocked the rifle: *click.* The sharp sound echoed across the marble floor. "If you don't get out of here, I'll kill you right along with her. You know I will."

Ariel bit her lip. He was serious; the flat monotone left no doubt. She glanced back at Leslie—who had slunk back against the wall, clutching the candle in trembling hands. The small flame flickered wildly.

"I—I don't get it," Ariel stammered, turning back to her brother. "Why are you after *Leslie?* She never did anything to you—"

"None of your damn business!" Trevor shouted. He lumbered forward. She could see his eyes now, half concealed under those brownish blond bangs . . . and they had the same lifeless quality she had seen in the eyes of those COFs who had attacked her. He raised the rifle and pointed it at Leslie. "Now get the hell out of here!"

But at that moment something in Ariel's brain snapped. Everything exploded at once: the hatred, the fear, the rage of being up *here* with her insane brother instead of down *there* partying, the loneliness at being shackled with some awful, unknown power that made people vaporize . . . but most of all, a fierce desire to protect Leslie. Leslie who had saved her life twice. Leslie who really cared about her. Leslie who stood by her and thought she was a good person. Leslie who behaved more like family than Ariel's own brother did.

Without thinking, she bolted across the hall and seized the cold metal barrel of the rifle with both hands.

"Get off!" Trevor screamed.

A deafening crack split the air next to her right ear. For a moment she couldn't hear anything but a high-pitched ringing. But she didn't stop. She kicked him hard in the shin. He cried out, and the gun faltered. With a vicious twist she wrenched it from his hands . . . then spun, allowing the momentum of her turn to carry her a full three-hundred-sixty degrees. . . . The rifle was a blur. Its butt smacked into Trevor's skull.

He screamed.

Then he sank to his knees.

"I hate you, Trevor!" Ariel shrieked, lifting the rifle again. "I should kill *you!*"

"No!" Leslie cried. "Ariel, stop!"

Ariel stood over her brother, eyes wide, rifle poised over her shoulder. Her lungs heaved. Blood was gushing from Trevor's temple. He clutched at his head, sniffling. Pathetic without his weapon. *Pathetic.* She wanted to hit him again and keep hitting him until he was out of her life forever. Until he could never hurt her—or anyone else—ever again.

"Go ahead!" he howled, bursting into tears. "Go

ahead and kill me! Do it! Kill me like you killed Mom!"

Like I what?

Ariel lowered the rifle and stared at him in astonishment. He wasn't in control of himself. He had turned into a raving lunatic.

"Kill me like you killed her," he sobbed.

"Uh . . . Trevor?" she muttered, struggling to catch her breath. "Why do you think I killed Mom?"

"Because you did." He collapsed to a fetal position on the floor. "I *saw* it," he wept. "I remember it."

Ariel gulped painfully. Why was he bringing up Mom? She'd never *seen* Trevor look so pitiful. "Trevor, Mom died in an accident, remember?" she murmured. "You were nine, and I was seven—"

"*I* remember!" he wailed. "Do *you?*" He raised his twisted face to hers. It was soaked in tears and half covered in blood. "What do you remember from that day? What do you *really* remember?"

Why are you doing this? Ariel wondered. She shook her head. A horrible, sick coldness spread through her body. She *hated* thinking about that day. The only thing she remembered was that she and her mom had gotten into a fight about something. And that was it. The rest was a fuzzy series of awful images, images she'd spent a lifetime trying to forget: an ambulance, a hospital room, a cemetery plot. She didn't *want* to argue with her mother. If Ariel had known she was going to die . . .

"I saw the whole thing," Trevor croaked. "Dad thought it was an accident, but he was wrong—he just couldn't face the truth about you. But I could. I hated you for it."

Ariel shook her head. "It's not true," she whispered.

But a terrible sense of dread was creeping up on her, smothering her.

It wasn't true. Trevor was making it up. He *had* to be. If it was true, wouldn't she remember? Why couldn't she *remember?*

"You make me sick," he spat. "The way Dad treated you better than me, the way you got away with everything, the way you had all those friends. Everybody thought you were so great. Nobody knew the truth but me—"

"And me," another voice finished.

Ariel's head jerked up.

Jezebel.

She walked out of the shadows of the stairwell and shook her head.

Ariel's head began to spin. Where had she come from? What was going *on* here?

Jezebel wasn't alone. Caleb was with her.

All the blood seemed to flow from Ariel's body, through the floor and into a black abyss.

No. God, no . . . this is some horrible lie.

"And now everybody knows the truth about who you are, Ariel," Jezebel stated coldly. *"Everybody."*

The Seventh Lunar Cycle

Naamah first saw the flashing signal sometime after midnight. It came from the desert hills near Harold Wurf's sleeping encampment: three quick bursts of light, followed by a long pause. The pattern was Lilith's code for an emergency.

For the first time in a very long while, Naamah felt afraid. She didn't understand it. Nothing was wrong. Every Visionary still believed that Harold Wurf was the Chosen One, that the tempest of blood had been a sign to march west. Nobody had any idea that Linda Altman was really Naamah, the high priestess of Lilith. Even Julia Morrison's doubts had been quashed. And even if they lingered, she had lost her will to fight. She was too concerned about her baby.

Perhaps somebody else was using that code by chance.

Perhaps it was an accident, a fluke. . . .

But when Naamah reached the light's source and

saw that it came from a silent helicopter silhouetted against the stars, she knew it was no mistake.

This was real.

"*Ki-si-kil-lil-la-ke*," an unseen voice hissed from the cockpit, using the ancient password.

"Naamah, the high priestess," Naamah whispered back.

A hooded sister hopped from the open door and scurried across the rocky terrain. Naamah trembled, squinting at her in the moonlight. The girl was holding something.

A cellular phone.

The sister stopped before Naamah and bowed her head. "I'm sorry to take such drastic measures. But we received the call tonight, and since we knew your exact location . . ." She handed Naamah the tiny device. "We don't have much time. The helicopter is due in Seattle in the morning."

Naamah's heart hammered as she brought the mouthpiece to her lips. "Hello?"

There was a crackle of static, and a soft voice answered: "It's Aviva."

Aviva? Naamah's eyes narrowed. What was this about? Naamah hadn't seen her since the attack in Russia, seven months ago. They weren't supposed to meet or talk again until the time of the Final Battle. Aviva was supposed to be mopping up Seers in the Middle East.

"I'm in the States," Aviva said. "I'm at Harold Wurf's farm."

"What . . . what are you doing there?" Naamah asked shakily.

Aviva laughed. "I was too far south when the Red Sea flooded. I had to improvise. I met up with Elijah Levy's grandniece."

"Sarah Levy!" Naamah cried. "But—"

"She survived the flood as well. And the scroll survived with her."

The scroll? Naamah's fear gave way to stark terror. "Wh-where is it?" she stammered.

"Don't worry," Aviva interrupted. "The scroll is safe with me. Sarah doesn't know I have it. She thinks it's at the bottom of the ocean."

Naamah gasped.

And slowly, very slowly . . . she smiled.

So it wasn't a crisis. No. It was a victory. The scroll was in the hands of the Lilum. The panic subsided, replaced with a familiar ecstasy—the ecstasy of triumph. She had resigned herself to losing the scroll forever. But once again the Lilum had prevailed. She was foolish to have given in to doubt.

"Naamah?" Aviva asked in the silence.

"I'm sorry," Naamah apologized, instantly slipping back into her role as leader. "Go on."

"I didn't mean to alarm you, but I thought I'd catch up with you in Texas. I ran into a few setbacks along the way. I apologize for using the emergency code, but I wanted to make sure I could pinpoint your exact location—and to make certain that you wouldn't go any farther."

Naamah nodded. "I understand. It will take you about a week to get here. I'll stall—"

"I can be there by the day after tomorrow," Aviva interrupted.

She frowned. "How? The helicopter is due on the West Coast."

"I have a chauffeur," Aviva said with a mischievous

chuckle. "A Seer named George Porter. Apparently he's good with cars."

"George Porter?" Naamah scowled. "But he vaporized."

"That's what he wanted you to think."

Naamah shook her head. A dozen questions sprang up in her mind . . . but there was no point in asking them now. They would all be answered soon enough.

"Instruct George to drive you and Sarah to the town plaza in Santa Fe, New Mexico. I don't care how you do it—seduce him if you have to," she commanded. "I'll be waiting there."

"Should I just dispose of Sarah?" Aviva asked.

"Not yet," Naamah answered. "She may be useful to us. But if she isn't, I'll take care of her and George myself. Both will make excellent burnt offerings to Lilith, don't you think?"

COUNTDOWN
to the
MILLENNIUM
Sweepstakes

$2,000 for the year 2000

5...4...3...2...1 MILLENNIUM MADNESS.
The clock is ticking ... enter now to win the prize of the millennium!

1 GRAND PRIZE:
$2,000 for the year 2000!

2 SECOND PRIZES: $500

3 THIRD PRIZES: balloons, noisemakers, and other party items (retail value $50)

Official Rules
COUNTDOWN
Consumer Sweepstakes

1. No purchase necessary. Enter by mailing the completed Official Entry Form or print out the official entry form from www.SimonSays.com/countdown or write your name, telephone number, address, and the name of the sweepstakes on a 3" x 5" card and mail it to: Simon & Schuster Children's Publishing Division, Marketing Department, Countdown Sweepstakes, 1230 Avenue of the Americas, New York, New York 10020. One entry per person. Sweepstakes begins November 9, 1998. Entries must be received by December 31, 1999. Not responsible for postage due, late, lost, stolen, damaged, incomplete, not delivered, mutilated, illegible, or misdirected entries, or for typographical errors in the entry form or rules. Entries are void if they are in whole or in part illegible, incomplete, or damaged. Enter as often as you wish, but each entry must be mailed separately.

2. All entries become the property of Simon & Schuster and will not be returned.

3. Winners will be selected at random from all eligible entries received in a drawing to be held on or about January 15, 2000. Winner will be notified by mail. Odds of winning depend on the number of eligible entries received.

4. One Grand Prize: $2,000 U.S. Two Second Prizes: $500 U.S. Three Third Prizes: balloons, noise makers, and other party items (approximate retail value $50 U.S.).

5. Sweepstakes is open to legal residents of U.S. and Canada (excluding Quebec). Winner must be 20 years old or younger as of December 31, 1999. Employees and immediate family

members of employees of Simon & Schuster, its parent, subsidiaries, divisions, and related companies and their respective agencies and agents are ineligible. Prizes will be awarded to the winner's parent or legal guardian if under 18.

6. One prize per person or household. Prizes are not transferable and may not be substituted except by sponsors, in event of prize unavailability, in which case a prize of equal or greater value will be awarded. All prizes will be awarded.

7. All expenses on receipt and use of prize, including federal, state, and local taxes, are the sole responsibility of the winners. Winners may be required to execute and return an Affidavit of Eligibility and Release and all other legal documents that the sweepstakes sponsor may require within 15 days of attempted notification or an alternate winner will be selected.

8. By accepting a prize, a winner grants to Simon & Schuster the right to use his/her name and likeness for any advertising, promotional, trade, or any other purpose without further compensation or permission, except where prohibited by law.

9. If the winner is a Canadian resident, then he/she will be required to answer a time-limited arithmetical skill-testing question administered by mail.

10. Simon & Schuster shall have no liability for any injury, loss, or damage of any kind, arising out of participation in this sweepstakes or the acceptance or use of a prize.

11. The winner's first name and home state or province will be posted on www.SimonSaysKids.com or the names of the winners may be obtained by sending a separate, stamped, self-addressed envelope to: Winner's List "Countdown Sweepstakes", Simon & Schuster Children's Marketing Department, 1230 Avenue of the Americas, New York, NY 10020.

Sarah.   Josh.

   Ariel.   Brian.

      Harold.   Julia.

         George.

Don't grow too attached to them.
They won't live long.

Don't miss the next thrilling installment of
Daniel Parker's

COUNTDOWN

AT BOOKSTORES EVERYWHERE

Printed in the United States
By Bookmasters